THE
LAST OWNERS

JEAN REZAB

For all the people who continue to work for those
in need, spiritually and physically

PROLOGUE
Eight Years Ago

"I buried the jewels."

Valerie looked up from the sink where she was washing carrots for the night's party. Simon stood by the island with dirt on his hands and jeans. His balding head glistened from exertion. She appreciated his efforts and looked forward to getting on the road tomorrow to their new future.

"Thanks, sweetie. I know you think I'm being too cautious, but I've been catching glimpses of envy from lots of women looking at my bracelets. I should have stuck to wearing only my watch and these earrings." She shook her head at her naïve belief. Small communities had criminals too.

"You're welcome. I'm as nervous about them as you are." Looking down at the dirt on his clothes, he backed away. "I've got the wooden box covered deep enough in the dirt, and no one will know something's buried there. I watered the ground. By the time everyone gets here this evening, the spot will look the same as the surrounding area. I'm going to clean up." He walked down the hallway to their bedroom suite.

Maybe her fear that someone would take this last opportunity to steal her jewelry was paranoia, but it was worth a lot of money. The community knew about her collection due to her unfortunate lapse in judgment. Several people commented on its value in the past few weeks. Simon understood her fears and had even kept his gun unpacked for the night. They'd dig up the jewelry in the morning and take it and the gun with them when they moved.

What was done was done. They needed to complete preparations for her and Simon's going-away party. She'd concentrate on enjoying the party this evening.

****

Sometime later that night, she woke to the sound of someone walking in their house. Simon slept soundly beside her, so she jabbed him in the side and whispered, "Someone's in the house."

He sat up abruptly, sliding quietly out of bed. He fumbled for the gun on the end table.

She slid out of bed, nerves jangling. All their possessions were outside in the RV, except the gun and her jewelry, which they'd buried until they were ready to leave in the morning.

Her instincts were right. Someone wanted her jewels. At least she'd told another person besides Simon where they were hidden. But now she regretted not sending the jewelry by registered mail to Virginia and letting everyone in town know.

The footsteps stopped in the hallway. She heard the squeak of a board, then nothing. Then, the screech of a sliding drawer in the study caused her heart to race. The intruder knew the layout of the house and hadn't hesitated.

Simon stole out of their bedroom and down the hall with her behind him. She peeked around his shoulder where he stood silently in the doorway of the study.

Two figures dressed in black, heads covered with masks, stood at the safe while one tried to open it. They must have sensed Valerie and

Simon's presence because one of them turned and pointed a flashlight directly at them.

"Open the safe," the intruder ordered.

Valerie couldn't tell if it was a man or woman. The gun in the other intruder's hand caused her to gasp. Her mouth went dry. She whispered in Simon's ear, "They have a gun."

He nodded, but his body trembled. Simon was a peaceable man. He wouldn't want to shoot them. He had the gun just to threaten, not to shoot.

Once, she'd shaken her head at him and told him shooting might be his only option. But he was ignoring her warning tonight.

"Move away from the safe and sit down in those chairs over there." He pointed to the chairs in front of the desk in the study. "I have a gun."

"So do we." The figures moved away from the safe and closer to Valerie and Simon. "We want the jewels, and we're not leaving without them."

The muffled voice was faintly familiar, but Valerie still couldn't decide if the low, quiet timbre was male or female. "They're not here." She stepped around Simon. "We mailed them to

Virginia." She clenched her perspiring hands together.

"I don't think so. We already checked the RV, and we didn't find them. That leaves the house. Where are they?" The person took another step toward them. The gun was pointed only a few feet from Valerie. "Tell me." She looked at Simon. "Or I'll shoot her."

"No, you won't."

Valerie heard the resolution in Simon's voice. What was going to happen? She wanted to close her eyes. Simon wouldn't let them kill her. He'd get them the jewelry first. But maybe he thought they'd give up and not really want to shoot anyone. That would be a mistake. She didn't think these two robbers cared. They'd shoot.

As she reached to take the gun from Simon with the intention of shooting in the direction of the burglars, he didn't resist at first. Then, he tightened his grip, realizing what she planned.

"No." His voice came out firmly. "I'll take care of it." He shot in the direction of the two figures.

Valerie knew he deliberately missed and hoped they'd run.

They didn't. The one in front shot Simon in the chest.

He groaned and dropped to the floor. Valerie leaned over him. Her heartbeat sounded in her ears.

She looked up at the figures, no longer feeling fear, but an anger so deep, she thought it would suffocate her.

"Give me the earrings and watch you're wearing." The shooter held out a gloved hand.

Valerie almost said no, but she didn't want the person touching her and taking them. After removing them, she dropped them on the floor beside the person's outstretched hand.

They would kill her no matter what she did. She wasn't telling them where the jewels were now.

CHAPTER 1
Eight Years Later
Wednesday, October 2nd

For the first time in a long time, Courtney thought about something other than the renovation of the house she and Alex planned to run as an inn. Sitting with her back to the counter and stools at Patty's Diner, the view outside the big windows stretched in front of her. With breakfast finished, the grant paperwork waited for her at home. The deadline approached, and they needed the money from the grant to complete the inn.

The two men in the corner booth joined her. One sat in the chair at her left, and the other sat on the chair across from him on Courtney's other side. Although Elm City was a small town, she'd never seen either man in the few weeks she and Alex had lived here. Surprised by their action, she couldn't believe she didn't feel threatened. What could they want? Courtney glanced over her shoulder at Patty, a silent question in her eyes.

Patty, her usual hair net holding back her bobbed brown hair, smiled back and filled a carafe of coffee. "I'll be right over to give you all a refill."

Relieved by Patty's warmth, she turned to the man on her left. "Can I help you?"

The bald guy—the leader?—appeared neatly groomed and smiled at her. "I'm Waylon Frederickson and work as a plumber. This is my brother, Johnny, who does electric work around the nearby counties."

A whiff of alcohol wafted from the bearded guy on the other side of her, who had a full head of dark hair and bleary eyes, suggesting he either had a long night or an early start this morning. He seemed to be the follower.

"They're twins." Patty threw the information into the conversation from back at the counter.

At the moment, they didn't look alike.

"They also have a younger sister, Lori." When Patty approached, Waylon jumped up to pull out the chair across from Courtney for her. "You don't have to do that," Patty scolded. "How many times do I have to tell you?"

Johnny's sudden smile lit up his face as he turned to Courtney. "Waylon always pulls out a chair for her or holds a door open. He does it to get a rise out of her, since she's usually so calm."

"It's the polite thing to do." Waylon scowled at Johnny before bowing to Patty. "Plus, she's special."

Spots of red appeared on Patty's cheeks as she sat down. Holding up the coffee pot, she asked, "Anybody need a refill?"

"No, thanks." The day's events had already ramped up Courtney's anxiety. Additional stimulus wasn't necessary. "How do you know each other, and why haven't we met before now?"

Patty turned over the coffee cups by each twin, filled them, and set the glass coffee pot on a potholder she'd brought along with the coffee. "We went to school together in the same grade. We're all approaching our big fortieth birthdays this year. You probably haven't needed their services yet in the few weeks you and Alex have been here, but you may in the future."

"Maybe. While the house we're renting is definitely old, it's not needed any electric or plumbing work yet. Not to be rude, but why have the two of you joined me?"

Patty chimed in, "They want a job. Right, boys?"

Courtney watched Waylon's jaw drop before snapping closed again. He glared at Patty. Johnny didn't stop chewing as he watched them.

Waylon's face now rivaled Patty's in redness. "Right."

"I'm Courtney Richmond," she said, "which I'm sure you know if you want a job. My husband, Alex, is out at the Miller house, preparing for the next stage of renovation."

She and Alex needed more help renovating the Miller house into their dream inn. If these guys could swing a hammer, do plumbing and electric work, they could help. Patty made sure Courtney knew the men wanted to work, so her recommendation was good enough. She would address the drinking if they decided to hire the brothers.

Waylon grinned. "I live on Sunflower Lane, down the street from you and Alex. Johnny lives a few streets away from me. You've rented the old Dodge house, right?"

"Yes. So, is Patty right? Do you want a job?"

"Generally, we pick up odd jobs to pay the bills. We're looking for something steadier for a change, but we'll continue doing odd jobs around town as people need them. Can't leave them in the lurch. Johnny is a licensed electrician. I can fix anything, while specializing in plumbing. I leave the electrical work to Johnny. We take jobs together."

"Always," Patty said.

Johnny frowned at her.

"Come on out to the inn about two o'clock this afternoon if you want a job. Alex and our forewoman, Honor, can talk to you, and we can all decide what to do. They get final say."

"We'll be there at two to see what they think," Waylon said.

Patty nodded her approval. "What's happening at the inn?"

Aware the other two occupants at the table listened with interest, Courtney kept her response to known facts. "I wouldn't call it an inn yet. The contractors finished the pre-demolition and put the temporary supports in place a few days ago.

Today and tomorrow, they're supposed to put in the permanent beams and supports. Alex is waiting for the final truck to arrive now, and then I'm going out there."

"What an exciting step forward." Patty clapped.

"It is." Courtney's phone rang, interrupting them, and she grabbed it from her pocket. "The last truck must have arrived."

"Hi, Alex. How's it going?" She expected a simple update.

"A little hiccup here at the site." His voice sounded strained. "A fire broke out—"

Picturing the house going up in flames, Courtney jumped up from her seat. "What? Was anyone hurt? How big? What are we going to do?"

"Hey, calm down." He spoke quietly. "Everyone's okay. Take a breath."

She followed his directions, her heart rate slowing to a more normal beat. "What happened?"

"A little accident with some rags. The fire's already extinguished. It's a small spot, and no harm done. The place is being remodeled, so it didn't cause any additional work. Maybe a six-foot square."

"How'd it start?" She dropped back into her chair, relieved.

"Working on that. Oh, I have to go. The last truck with the beams is pulling in, and the fire inspector has come out to take a look. We called the fire department but cancelled when we extinguished the fire ourselves. However, the inspector needs to check it out."

A fire inspector? What happened out there? "I'll be out in a few minutes." Fortunately, the inn was only three miles from Elm City. Her curiosity wouldn't take long to be satisfied.

She hung up and regarded the three people who had listened to her call. "A minor fire, I'm sure the gossip mill will report in due time, but you heard it here first. No harm done."

The brothers exchanged a glance.

She'd have to follow up later with Patty. They seemed to know something. "I need to run now. Hope to see you guys at two. Thanks, Patty." She stood and dropped some cash from her jeans pocket on the table. She waved at them on her way to the exit.

"Take care, Courtney," Patty called after her. "Everything will be fine."

Would it? What would cause rags to catch fire? Smoking wasn't allowed in the building. Had someone set it deliberately? Why would the idea even cross her mind?

From the road, she couldn't tell any difference to the outside of the inn. It looked the same as yesterday. She arrived on the scene as a driver got back into a truck that hadn't been at the inn the previous night. Must have dropped off the new beam.

She parked out of the way to leave room for everyone to maneuver. No one had taken care of the area for eight years since the Millers left. Their son, Gary, who'd sold them the place, had someone mow a large area around the building for them.

The activity from the renovation showed in all the tire tracks and trodden weeds and grass. Stacks of lumber piled in various places around the yard waited for disposal. The reusable lumber remained inside to keep it safe from the weather.

She stepped through the front door, greeted by the unmistakable scent of smoke, sawdust, and sweat. The hot October day heated the place. A few fans ran where the generator's electricity could be on without causing a problem. The renovation was in full swing, with workers bustling around, each immersed in their tasks.

Courtney heard the rhythmic hammering of nails and the low hum of electric saws slicing through wood. The sound of progress.

Carefully making her way to where Alex stood deep in conversation with the contractor from Dickinson, she waited patiently for a break in their discussion. Gazing around and not seeing any sign of where the fire took place, she took a breath of the stale air and relaxed. He'd told her the damage was minimal.

Finally, Alex finished and excused himself from the contractor. "Hey, Courtney. You want to see where the fire happened?" He led her to the far corner of what had been the living room.

She noticed a black charred spot about a foot long and a few inches wide. She gazed at him in confusion.

"Yeah, a small scare. No real damage done," he replied. "I wish we knew before calling the fire department. Now there's going to be paperwork."

She shook her head and tapped his arm. "You did the right thing. It could have gotten out of hand and caused more damage, not to mention someone could have been hurt. Better to be safe. Where are the rags you mentioned that caught fire?"

"The inspector took them, so we wait for his report."

Frowning at the wait, she asked, "How is everything else going?"

Alex's face lit up. "It's coming along nicely. The new beams arrived this morning, and we're focusing on getting them installed in the next couple of days as planned."

Courtney glanced around, her mind drifting back to the fire. "Something's bothering me about the incident. Smoking isn't allowed, so what could have caused those rags to ignite?"

Alex frowned, rubbing his chin. "Could be anything. I'm letting the fire inspector decide. For now, let's focus on getting the beams in place."

She nodded, trying to focus.

Honor, the forewoman from the local company, asked her and Alex to leave the building, along with her husband, Doug. The men contracted from Dickinson had their own foreman and continued their work with the beams. Outside, the four of them stood and looked at each other.

Honor's husband worked for her on the renovation crew. How did Doug like working for his wife? None of the other men had any problem reporting to Honor, which relieved Courtney. Honor had earned her way in Elm City.

"What do we do while they work?" Courtney paced as she considered all the things she could be doing at the house on Sunflower Lane. Such as more paperwork for the grant offering funding for applicable projects. She was praying they fell into the right category. She needed to focus on it whenever she could.

Honor shrugged and reached into one of the coolers on the side of the house in the shade. "I'm waiting here to see if they need anything. Doug will back me up." She pulled out a bottle of water. "Anybody else want something to drink?"

Courtney and Alex both nodded, but Doug shook his head. "I'm going to the truck to check my messages and return calls."

Honor nodded as she grabbed two more waters and handed them around. "You can leave this crew to their work and come back later. They don't need our input. That's why we hired this outfit. Or maybe we can discuss some of the things we need to start on next Monday when these guys finish."

Courtney pushed her hair behind her ears. She'd allowed the color to go back to its natural brunette instead of keeping the purple highlights. It had grown down to her shoulders. She pulled a scrunchie out of her pocket and put it in a ponytail. The weather made it too hot to hang loose on her neck. At least the weather would be cooling off soon, since it was October.

"Maybe we can talk about a few more workers for the project." Courtney decided now would be a good time to bring up the Fredericksons' offer. "I found a potential plumber and electrician this morning. Or I should say, Patty found them."

Alex's brows rose. "That's Honor's domain."

Honor didn't appear upset. "Who do you have in mind?"

They all watched Doug as he opened the truck door then slammed it shut before he came to rejoin them.

"Johnny and Waylon Frederickson were at the diner this morning, and Patty—"

Doug broke in with a laugh. "You want to hire those two losers? Johnny's always drinking. Everyone knows. They hate working with him. And Waylon follows him around like his nanny."

Honor gasped. "Doug! That was cruel. I'll handle this. That's my job."

His face flushed at the reminder, and he stormed off to the truck without another word. Silence followed his exit.

Honor looked at Alex and Courtney. "Johnny does have a drinking problem, but he never drinks on the job. We should hire them. They're great at what they do."

"As long as he gets the job done right when he's here, I don't care. Everyone deserves a second chance," Alex assured Honor.

Courtney nodded. "It's Honor's decision. Patty recommended them, which is good enough for me."

"Let's hire them." Honor rubbed her hands against her jeans. "There are some considerations with those two. They only take jobs together. You get them as a pair. Must be because they're twins.

"As I said, they do good work. But Johnny drinks too much and misses work sometimes. As long as we factor that into the equation, it won't slow down the project. We could use their help, and I trust them. Waylon will keep an eye on Johnny and not let him work if he's not competent. I know we agreed I'd have the final say on hiring, but I'm leaving this one in your court. I'm fine either way." Honor waited quietly for their answer.

Courtney and Alex exchanged glances. Their business partners, Clarissa and Hugh, were taking a chance with them on building this inn.

Alex touched her shoulder. "Let's take a chance."

"I still haven't changed my mind. It's fine." She remembered Alex's jail term. He hadn't embezzled like everyone thought, even though he spent two years in prison. He was big on giving second chances, and she agreed with him.

"Okay." Courtney patted Alex's hand, which lay on her shoulder. "They'll be here at two for an interview, so if you and Honor are available to talk to them and set the ground rules, they can start next Monday if their schedule is open." Courtney glanced around. "There's nothing I can do here. I should go home and work on some of the grant paperwork."

Honor nodded. "I'll hang around and keep an eye on things."

"Me too." Alex fanned himself and took a gulp of water. "If Doug wants to leave, let him go. There's nothing he can do except get hot."

"I'll let him know." Honor left to talk to Doug.

Courtney leaned forward and kissed Alex on the cheek. "Give me a call if something comes up. The fire didn't cause much damage, but I still don't understand how it started."

"Let's not worry. We'll wait for the investigator to check those rags. It's probably something simple."

"You're right." She needed to take his advice.

He kissed her on the cheek in return. "Go home and cool off."

"I wish. The room air conditioner doesn't do much for the whole house." She couldn't wait for the new apartment to be finished on the second floor of the inn. "I'll concentrate on our dream inn. Real heat and air conditioning." She gazed around at the debris. "We'll have to get this stuff cleaned up before the snow falls."

"After this week, we can store more inside the inn, clean this up, and put a few bushes in front of the inn. The rest can wait until spring."

"Okay. You take care and stay safe." She waved as she got into her truck and drove away. Doug followed behind in his truck, obviously deciding he had no reason to stay either.

She cranked up the air conditioner and directed the vents toward her arms, wondering about the chances Honor would hire Johnny and Waylon. She seemed on board with the idea. As she drove toward Elm City, Doug's vehicle following, they met the fire inspector's truck going back to the inn.

She made a U-turn in the middle of the road. She wanted to know what started the fire.

CHAPTER 2

The fire inspector stood outside with Alex and Luke, the structural foreman, and Honor. Courtney joined them.

"So, the rags were cotton fabric with nothing flammable on them?" Alex asked.

"Right. A cigarette inside caused the fire. Someone didn't extinguish it before dropping it on the rags." The inspector stared at them. "We still need to determine if it was done intentionally."

Courtney looked at Alex in alarm, but she noticed Luke glancing at his men.

Luke shook his head. "Accidental. I know my men and who's responsible. He didn't think things through before he dropped the cigarette. I'm betting he dropped it, thought if he stepped on it quickly, it would go out, and no one would ever find out. He didn't realize the fabric would leap into flames at that spark before he could stop it. Let me get him."

Not waiting for a response, he walked to the door, opened it, and yelled, "Richie!"

Since the doors were glass and a lot of windows fronted the building, she saw a young guy glance up. His reddish-blond hair stuck to his forehead, where it showed beneath his hardhat. His white complexion turned red, and he looked around as if ready to run.

"Definitely him," Courtney whispered to Alex.

When Luke waved him outside, he walked as if to his execution. "What's up, Boss?" His voice shook.

"The cigarette."

Richie's freckled face whitened under his tan. "I did it. I guess you know. I'm sorry. I didn't realize dropping the cigarette would start the rags on fire. I thought the flame would be smothered, and I'd stomp on it to be sure."

He closed his eyes as if in agony. "I wasn't quick enough. I'm sorry." He gazed around at the group. "Really sorry."

"We know. You can go back to work." Luke patted him on the back before Richie headed inside. "Any charges to process?"

"No." The fire inspector marked something down on the clipboard he held. "Sounds like an accident, but I'd make sure he doesn't do it again."

She hadn't met the fire inspector. "I'm Courtney Richmond." She held out her hand. "Owner of the property with Alex."

"Max Stoddart." He shook her hand. "Do you and Mr. Richmond want to press charges?"

She didn't. She looked at Alex.

"Nope. We're good here." Alex's face relaxed when he found out it wasn't sabotage but an accident. A smile tilted his lips. "Thanks for doing all this work over something so minor."

"I don't exactly consider any fire minor." Max Stoddart stood, looking down at his feet before lifting his head and staring sternly at those assembled. "They can turn nasty fast. You were lucky here." He fixed his gaze on Luke. "Tell the kid not to smoke around here. We don't want any prairie fires. A bit of wind, and a fire can get out of control and take out a lot of acres."

"I'll remind all the men they need to wait to get home to smoke. It's a rule they shouldn't break. Richie's new, but he'll know now too."

Courtney gave him credit for not denigrating Richie in front of them. The guy appeared barely old enough to have a job, and he worked on Luke's team. He must be good at what he did.

The fire inspector took off, and Luke went back in to supervise. Alex, Honor, and Courtney remained outside.

"Thank goodness it was an accident." Honor rubbed her hands against her jeans again. "I thought we were going to have to deal with a saboteur."

"I hear there's some story about a disappearance from this house." Courtney wanted Honor's opinion of what happened to the Millers.

Honor jerked back.

Courtney caught the slight action because she'd been watching closely. She was curious to find out Honor's version compared to the gossip in town. "What happened?"

When they bought the house from the Millers' son, Gary, she promised him they would gather any information they could about his parents while they renovated the house. He told her it could be dangerous, but Courtney's curiosity edged out her concern. The mysterious disappearance captured her attention. Alex wasn't happy she was so eager to play detective, and he'd probably be proven right, but he didn't object.

"The previous owners disappeared in the middle of the night." Honor shrugged at the vagaries of people. "Sold their jewelry and disappeared."

"Jewelry?" Courtney pretended ignorance. Gary told her he hoped his parents were still alive, but he hadn't found any sign of them in eight years. He thought the jewels were probably stolen, and his parents killed for them. He continued hoping and searching.

Honor's hands clenched into fists. "There was some speculation Valerie, Mrs. Miller, owned a lot of jewelry from her time in New York before they moved here. Rubies, sapphires, emeralds, and diamonds. Valerie wore different bracelets, and there were rumors she had matching necklaces. I saw one necklace. That's all. It was eight years ago."

"A long time to remember who mentioned they'd seen them all," Alex agreed.

Honor rubbed her construction boot into the dirt. "There may have only been one necklace."

She lifted her head and met Courtney's eyes. "Anyway, next week when the construction crew gets back on the grounds, we'll keep an eye out in case something happened to the Millers here. The crew might believe jewels are hidden somewhere on the grounds, and we don't want them digging around instead of working. They might be hoping they'll make a big find. The group here today doesn't know anything about the history of the place, so you're safe from snooping until they leave."

"Some people think the Millers never left?" Courtney asked.

Honor frowned. "Where the jewels are concerned, everybody wants to cash in. Who doesn't love the idea of finding buried treasure, right? They keep ignoring the fact the Millers' RV was found in South Dakota. I'm sure they would have taken the jewelry with them, if she really had a big collection. Now, I should get back to work."

Courtney didn't point out they couldn't do anything but wait. She was more interested in Honor's uncomfortable responses.

While they'd been talking, Doug stood there without speaking. For some reason, he'd returned to the construction site while they talked to the fire inspector. Maybe because he saw her do a U-turn. "Imagine the finder's fee if it's true the jewels are buried on the property."

"Are we going to have problems with treasure hunters?" Alex asked Honor.

Honor shrugged. "It could go either way."

"We'll deal with whatever happens." Courtney wouldn't let anybody come between her and her dream inn. "Tell us what people in town said when it happened. We heard the Millers' RV was packed and parked in front of the house the evening before they planned to leave. Then what?"

Honor nodded agreement. "The next morning, they were gone. The RV and Valerie and Simon. Everyone assumed they'd taken off early in the morning as planned. There wasn't any sign of anything out of the ordinary.

"We all went about our business. One day, the sheriff got a call saying the Millers never arrived at their new home in Virginia. The previous owners of their new property in Virginia tried to contact them with no luck. About a week later, police found the RV down in some ravine in

South Dakota. They assumed they'd find Valerie's and Simon's bodies in the RV or at the bottom of the ravine. But after some recovery work of the vehicle, they didn't find either of them. So they assumed Valerie and Simon took off and were hiding for some reason, or they'd met with foul play somewhere along the way.

"When the previous owners of the Virginia house found out Valerie and Simon had a son in the Air Force who couldn't make it home to help, they agreed to rent a storage unit for the possessions in the Virginia house. From what Valerie and Simon told us, the house was almost fully furnished, and they'd traveled there a few times to get the place ready for their arrival. Technically, the house belonged to Valerie and Simon, and the money had gone through for the sale, which re-enforced the belief the Millers were wealthy."

Honor shrugged. "That's about it. We all assume their son inherited everything when he went through the process of having his parents declared deceased. They haven't been seen since the night they left this house."

"That must have been hard for Gary, not knowing what happened and being unable to get out of his military duties to investigate." Courtney couldn't imagine if her parents disappeared.

When they bought the property, Gary told Courtney and Alex he searched for his parents whenever he had leave from the military, but he'd had no luck. He hated declaring them dead, but he needed to be the owner so he could sell the property. She didn't envy him. He said if his parents ever showed up, he'd make it right with them.

She liked Gary. He'd become a deputy sheriff here in the county, hoping to get further information on what happened. The fact his parents were last seen alive in Elm City brought him to the conclusion they might never have left, and the RV in South Dakota was a distraction from the truth. His desperation for closure led him to ask her and Alex to do a little safe sleuthing. He made it clear they should be subtle and quit if their questions caused danger.

Alex had laughed and assured Gary that Courtney couldn't do subtle. He meant well, but she was perturbed he was right.

Gary more than qualified as deputy after his military training. He'd hoped to keep a low profile, so he could investigate his parents' disappearance. He didn't hide the fact the Millers were his parents, but he didn't advertise it either. With his last name being Lachlan, it wasn't obvious. He'd kept his biological father's name when Simon Miller adopted him. He'd told Courtney, in a small community like Elm City, it was nearly impossible to keep it secret.

Luke came outside, along with the rest of his crew. "Going well in there. Break time."

Alex smiled at him. "No need to explain."

"I'm used to keeping the client happy." He grinned. "You two have been my easiest clients in a long time." His look included Honor. "And you too, of course."

A scowl crossed Doug's face at the compliment, but he stayed silent.

Courtney noted Doug's jealousy. How long had he and Honor been married? Would it last with Honor as the boss?

Courtney spoke to Luke. "Because we don't know anything to contradict what you're doing. Plus, you came with excellent references."

A frown marred Luke's tanned face. "Except when I have someone smoke on the job."

"Forget it. I'm sure he won't do it again. No harm done." Relieved it was an accident, she wanted to move on.

"What's the timeline now?" Honor asked.

Courtney was grateful for the subject change.

"We'll be out of here by noon Friday. Maybe even tomorrow evening." He looked up at the sky. "These shorter daylight hours make it harder to keep going too late."

"I love October, but it isn't usually this hot." Courtney wiped her sweaty palms against her jeans and realized that was what Honor had been doing. Was it an indication of when Honor felt nervous? She'd have to watch and see. "I do agree about the darkness coming on too soon."

"Well, there isn't any problem getting done on time." Luke glanced around at them and settled on Honor. "Anything else we can do before we're done this week?"

"No. Thanks. It's been great working with your professionals. I love my crew here, but I don't get to keep them all year long." She laughed. "Too much fieldwork."

"But you love it." Happiness rang in Courtney's words.

"I do. Ever since I watched the first remodeling TV show when I was young, I knew this was my destiny." Her relaxed face showed satisfaction. "We're fine, Luke. Go take your break."

He stepped away and joined a few of the guys sitting on the tailgate of a nearby pickup.

"He's something." Admiration tinged Honor's words. "Maybe someday I can move to a bigger city and do what he does."

"You can," Courtney encouraged her. "I never thought I'd be getting my dream inn to help people get their lives together, but look at this. I've always wanted to set up a place where people could stay for a week and consider a big life choice they're facing. Whether it's divorce, a death, a change in job…this helps them take time to think on it in a neutral place. I can't wait until our deacon and psychologist join us. This renovation means my dream is coming true. It's happening."

Honor stood up straighter. "You're right. I'll make it happen."

Doug smirked. "Well, we've got a long way to go."

"Spoiler." She didn't sound happy with him.

"Okay. Alex and Honor, don't forget Johnny and Waylon will be here around two o'clock." Courtney had her answer and was ready to go home.

"The western duo. Their mother has such a love for country music, all her children are named for country stars. Waylon Jennings, Johnny Cash, and Loretta Lynn. The daughter refuses to answer if called Loretta, so she goes by Lori." Doug rolled his eyes.

"Interesting." A glint appeared in Alex's eyes. "Who's your favorite singer?" he asked Courtney.

She shook her head at him. She knew where he was headed. No way were they naming any children after music icons—unless it was accidental.

On her way back to town, she remembered the call she'd gotten from Gary asking if he could bring a cadaver dog to the inn to search for his parents. She'd agreed. As soon as the structural crew finished, Gary would bring in the dog. She'd text Alex when she got home.

CHAPTER 3
Friday, October 4th

The structural work finished Thursday evening. Courtney and Alex agreed to meet Honor on Friday afternoon to review the plans one more time. The local workers would be starting their work on Monday, including their new hires, Johnny and Waylon.

Courtney and Alex arrived at the quiet construction site. They wanted to wander inside the quiet building in the morning before Gary came with the dog.

The open space echoed without the construction workers. They'd removed a lot of walls that weren't in the right place for the inn's layout. She headed to look out the back door to view the rear of the property. Before they'd started demolition and renovation, they mowed a wide patch around the building.

"How should we do the backyard? I'm planning lots of flowers and bushes next spring instead of this short, brown dry grass. We can plant those evergreens along the edge of the backyard this fall. The guys are coming next week to put them in place."

When she opened the back door, she gasped. "And holes to fill in. Lots of holes." She stared at rows and rows across the backyard. Each row was about a yard from the next row. The holes appeared about a foot deep and a foot in circumference.

Alex came to stand beside her at the doorway. "Lots of holes."

Courtney pressed her forehead against the window. "What are those doing in the backyard? It looks like a badger went around digging for something last night."

"They weren't there when I left last evening. They appear similar in size and distance from each other. Kind of like someone searching for something." He and Courtney exchanged glances.

"Jewels," they chorused.

He opened the door to step outside before remembering there were no steps down to the yard. The deck and back steps decayed over the years, and the old, rotted wood had been removed.

The drop to the ground was far enough to be unsafe to jump down.

As Courtney rushed out the front door and around to the back of the building, Alex followed. They stood at the perimeter of the mown grass, staring at the black holes dotting the landscape.

He walked around, peering inside the shallow holes about twelve inches deep, deep enough to know someone hadn't hidden anything in the spot, unless they'd dug even deeper. "It's possible whoever did this last night will be back to dig deeper or in a different area."

"They knew there wouldn't be any workers here today."

"Which doesn't exclude anybody since this project is the talk of the town. Anyone could have mentioned it at the bar last night, and someone overheard, and soon the information went all over town and country."

Courtney nodded. Someone had plenty of time to hear the news and come here last night. They might have even assumed no one would visit the site until Monday when work started again. "Do we call the sheriff's office?"

"Yes. If they start breaking into the building and doing damage to the walls, we need this on record. Plus," he waved his hand across the backyard area, "they were determined. The holes so close together cover the whole area. The earth is dry and hard—those took some muscle to dig. I figure eighty to one hundred holes."

After calling the sheriff's office, they spent more time inside, making sure nothing was disturbed. Not finding anything out of the ordinary, they assumed the person hadn't gone inside the building. Maybe they planned for another time, as Alex believed. Right now, only she, Alex, and Honor had keys to the building.

Courtney found herself shaking. Annoyance warred with the knowledge this was going to be a long, drawn-out battle to renovate the house into an inn. If someone started destroying the inside of the building to find the jewels, the construction workers would spend all their time redoing what they'd already done.

Deputy Gary Lachlan arrived first from the sheriff's office—the Millers' son and seller of the house. They went out to meet him, surprised he wasn't in uniform. He'd planned to bring the dog with him. Gary was in his thirties, bald, with a thin and wiry build.

When he got out of the car, he stood at the SUV's door, where the dog flicked her tail and looked out the window.

Courtney admired the retriever. "You aren't working today?"

"Sheriff Warren agreed I could search as arranged this morning, but I can't be in uniform because it involves my parents. The sheriff told me what happened and wanted me to continue with my plan to search the area. He's wanted to know what happened to my parents as long as I have." Gary let the dog out of the car and leashed her. "Her name is Rain."

"She's gorgeous. Can I pet her?"

Gary nodded.

She couldn't think of him as a deputy when he was dressed in civilian clothes, and they'd spent time working with him to buy the house. He'd explained then about his parents and how he searched for them. It brought him to Elm City. He figured they'd never left the farm.

The Labrador retriever's fur was glossy, golden, and soft as Courtney smoothed her hand down Rain's side and scratched her head. "She's beautiful. You take great care of her."

"She's not my dog." He stood watching her pet Rain. His hands clenched.

Her head jerked up.

"She belongs to a friend of mine. I asked if I could borrow Rain today, and Wendy agreed. We're not going very far, and I'll take Rain back when we finish today. She trusts me." He rubbed his hand along the back of his neck.

"Oh, Gary." Courtney wanted to pat him like she had the dog. He brought in a cadaver dog—he must have believed his parents were dead.

"I'm waiting for the sheriff. He agreed to let Rain search the backyard where the holes were dug first. I gave him a heads-up last week when there was a break in construction, I'd bring Rain to search the property. Now someone else has dug here, he wants to see the ground before Rain walks around."

Alex slapped him gently on the back. "Let's pray you get an answer soon."

Gary shrugged. "I don't pray much since I left the Air Force. Too busy."

Alex grinned, but then the smile slipped from his face. "But you weren't too busy in the Air Force? When we get some things taken care of here, we're going to have a talk about how long it takes to pray."

Gary began pacing. "Sounds like a good idea. I have lots of questions about my time in the service, and why my parents disappeared. Lots of things I want an answer about from God. Maybe you can steer me in the right direction."

"Any time it works for you, I'll drop everything and discuss what I've experienced, and what I know. Plus, I can bring in reinforcements." He smiled. "Not to push you or anything."

Gary's laugh sounded forced. "Right. Shouldn't the sheriff be here by now?"

Courtney kept stroking Rain's fur. "He'll come soon." She went with his change of subject. "Why don't you tell us what you think happened? Alex and I won't say anything."

He stopped in front of them and rubbed the back of his neck again. "I'm not sure if they were digging for jewels…or bones."

"Oh." The breath went out of Courtney. She stopped petting Rain and crossed her arms against the sudden chill sliding through her body. "I assumed the digger was someone who wanted to find the jewels."

The reality of having a cadaver dog finally sank in. Rain might find Gary's parents. She felt bad for him.

Opening the inn after finding bodies on the property wouldn't be helpful for the business either. How selfish was she? She would worry about the inn later.

"Or, if they killed my parents and buried them in the backyard, they might have come back to find the bodies and move them. I'm leaning toward the jewels, because they'd know what part of the yard they buried my parents in. They wouldn't be digging around the whole area." He gazed down at Rain. "We'll see soon."

"Because they dug back there doesn't mean your parents are buried there. They probably took off to live their life somewhere else." She tried to encourage him to believe his parents were alive.

"They would never have taken off without contacting me for eight years. I've believed they were dead since someone found the RV in the ravine. It makes the most sense. I followed their trail until it ended in South Dakota. They should have been easy to find. I'm good at tracking from my time in the military."

The sheriff pulled into the driveway.

"After that, I knew they'd never left the farm under their own power in the first place. Someone else drove their RV. Whether they took my parents somewhere else or left them here, I don't know, which is why I'm searching here now."

"We support you," Alex told him as the sheriff got out of the vehicle.

"Hi, Deputy." They shook hands. The sheriff was a man in his sixties with gray hair touched with a little youthful brown. He appeared to keep in good physical shape. He held his hand out to Courtney next. "You must be Mrs. Richmond."

She nodded and found she liked the firm handshake and kind look in the man's eyes. She knew it was for Gary's benefit, but that was okay.

Alex held his hand out, and the sheriff shook it. "Mr. Richmond."

"You can call us Alex and Courtney," Alex told him. "Gary's already told us about Rain, and we're fine with a brief search of the backyard. I'm hoping we can have you and Gary out of here before Doug and Honor get here. I'd like to keep the investigation among the four of us."

"Gary, why didn't you bring Rain in sooner?" Courtney would have brought in a cadaver dog right away if her parents were missing.

"I wanted to see if anybody let down their guard and did anything hinting my parents never left Elm City. If I'd brought in Rain sooner, they would have been put on guard. It didn't net me any information.

"I've learned the guest list from my parents' party the night before they left the house. Those people are at the top of my suspect list. Nothing else stands out to me except the constant reference to jewelry whenever my parents are mentioned. Everyone I talked to in town gushed over my mom's bracelets and rings. They said she wore them around town a lot. Now, since someone dug back here, it gives me a place to start."

The sheriff nodded. "I was in on the plan. Between the structural crew and Honor's crew working next week, Gary planned to get Rain for today and talk to the two of you to get your approval."

"We planned on getting more information first from further questioning of people who might know more about what happened, but this opportunity came up. I was going to call you and Alex today after I got here." Gary patted Rain. "But when I got here, you showed me someone had already been here last night. Whoever they are, they had the same idea to come between work crews. I meant to give you more warning about Rain and see what you thought today. Now we have these holes. The person who dug them sped up the process."

Or Gary had taken advantage. She wondered for a minute if Gary was digging in the middle of the night. No. He wouldn't. The sheriff wouldn't stand in the way of Gary bringing in Rain, nor would she and Alex. They all supported Gary's use of a cadaver dog.

The sheriff stepped forward. "Let's go check out this digging situation, and Gary can get out of here before we start in the house."

The thoroughness of the sheriff's plan satisfied all parties involved. They hurried around to the backyard, taking in the rectangular space mowed between the house and a rundown shed.

"I'm sending a quick text to Honor and Doug to tell them not to come here. We'll meet at the Elm City house this afternoon instead." Courtney finished sending the text. "I should have done that sooner." She hurried to catch up with them.

Gary and Alex stood on the edge of the mowed area with Rain. The sheriff wandered around gazing at the holes, peering into every indentation. Thorough. Courtney approved.

Gary whispered something to Rain. Courtney assumed some kind of directions or preparations to get her in the cadaver dog mood. She'd have to explore how cadaver dogs worked sometime.

The sheriff finally came back to them and nodded to Gary. The tension in the atmosphere increased.

Gary commanded Rain to search, and she slowly walked along beside him as he led her from hole to hole.

CHAPTER 4

"We'll start the search back here by the shed and go toward the house." Gary let Rain lead the way and turned her at the next row of holes. "If anything is buried, they would have done it along the back area here by the shed instead of up by the house."

Courtney thought Gary's idea was a good one. "Maybe we'll have to take Rain around the shed for good measure."

Silence fell as they watched Rain and Gary.

Courtney's heart beat faster and faster. If something was buried, Rain wouldn't find it. Unless it was Gary's parents. She didn't know what to hope for. Closure for Gary. Or Rain finding nothing, and Gary still having hopes his parents were alive. She couldn't imagine the anxiety of her own parents missing for eight years.

Suddenly, Rain circled a hole in the middle of the yard and sat down beside it, staring at the area.

A collective sigh sounded among the watchers.

"You got a red stick marker, Gary?" the sheriff asked softly.

Gary nodded, his face unreadable. He pulled a red stick from his pants pocket and stuck it in the dirt. He patted Rain, called her to him and gave her a treat. They continued searching the rest of the yard with no further reaction from Rain.

"We should try around the shed now." Sheriff Warren started walking toward the back of the yard where the shed barely remained standing.

Gary nodded and led Rain around the shed, while the rest of them stood where they waited before. "Nothing," he called out. "Except there is another hole dug back here."

They went to the back of the shed. The sheriff held out his hand to stop Alex and Courtney from coming closer, and Gary and Rain joined them at the corner.

"I'm guessing someone knew something was here. They came right to this spot, dug it out and left. The hole here is deeper than the others in the yard."

Courtney stared at the location of the hole. "It's about halfway between the tree and the shed. They probably used it as their guide."

"I don't get it. If it was the jewels, why didn't your parents take them with them instead of leaving them in the ground?" Alex asked.

"My guess, they didn't get a chance to come back here and get them in the morning." Gary's mouth firmed into a straight line. "Someone knew. My parents trusted and told them about the jewels. For some reason, they waited until recently to retrieve them. I'm not sure why they would have left them here this long. That hole looks pretty fresh. Unless they thought this was the safest place for them. They were worth a lot of money. Maybe a million dollars."

"Maybe they were waiting for someone to give them to." Courtney watched Gary's face light up. "You. Maybe someone dug them up to give to you. They waited for some sign of safety. Or they were afraid they'd be arrested if they turned them in—maybe afraid you'd think they stole them."

The other three shrugged.

"My mother was a little eccentric. I like to think she had someone besides my dad who she trusted." Gary smiled briefly. "Only she would bury her jewels instead of putting them in a safe in the house. Especially in a state where the ground freezes in the winter, and snow could pile up in that spot. If that's what she did. She said a safe inside the house would be an obvious place to keep important things, so, growing up in our New York house, I'd find her favorite things in odd places."

"Too much speculation and no evidence. We don't know if the jewels were buried. Let's see if someone brings them to us soon." The sheriff followed his path back to where everyone stood. "We've done what we could. I'm going to dig a little where Rain alerted. Not far down but enough to see if I find anything. I need something dull like a wooden spoon that won't damage anything."

Courtney turned to Alex. "Let's see if anyone left a toolbox with something inside hard enough to dig in the dirt but not too sharp." She placed a hand on Gary's arm as she walked past him, leaving him with the sheriff.

When they were inside, where they couldn't be heard, she said, "That could be his parents out there."

Alex's face somber, he nodded. "We'll know in a week or so."

She stopped her search for a tool and stared at him. "Why so long?"

"They're not going to be recognizable."

Nodding, she continued searching. "But I'm sure Gary has dental records on file. That'll shorten the time. We're talking like there's a body, and we haven't even seen bones yet."

"You're right. Let's hurry."

They found a screwdriver, and the end of the rubber handle would work to move dirt gently. Taking it back out to the men, she found them talking earnestly together, but they went silent when she appeared with Alex.

"That'll work." Sheriff Warren took it from her and went to the red peg.

The others stood watch on the edge of the mowed area. Gary crossed his arms against his chest, and Rain sat quietly with her nose on his shoe. Giving comfort. Courtney found herself twisting her fingers together, and Alex reached over to hold one of them.

The waiting was almost worse than watching Rain search the area.

Finally, the sheriff stood up from his crouch and joined them. "I see a bone."

Gary's shoulders drooped, and he lowered his gaze to Rain. "Just one?"

The sheriff gazed at the hole. "Could be more. I'm not going to mess up what could be a crime scene. No more digging from me. Time for forensics."

Courtney didn't see the bone from her position along the sidelines.

Gary turned to Courtney and Alex. "Thanks for allowing us to search. I'm sure it's them, but…"

The sheriff's dig marks appeared fresh against the surrounding area.

Courtney glanced over at Gary, who met her gaze with a grimace. "Gary." She stepped closer. "There's something I need to ask."

An emotion she couldn't identify flickered in his eyes.

"Are we sure what Rain found is human? I mean, couldn't it be an animal bone? Maybe a pet they buried in their backyard?"

He slowly shook his head. "Rain knows the difference. I'm pretty sure it's them. After all this time. I've lived with the worst-case scenarios since they disappeared. It was a long shot to believe they're alive, but hope dies hard, even after eight years."

"Are you *sure* it isn't a pet they buried?" Courtney asked.

"My father was allergic to cats, and my mom didn't want to walk a dog. They liked being free to travel when they felt the urge."

"Maybe the previous owners—"

Gary interrupted her, "It's them."

As they stood in the backyard, the tension increased.

"Okay." She wasn't helping with her suggestions. Time to be quiet. Gary obviously had geared himself up for handling the worst outcome.

The sheriff glared at them. "It looks like a finger bone. I didn't tell you. Right?"

They all nodded.

Gary observed the sheriff. "How long until someone can get here and determine if it's them?"

"Somewhere between a few days to a week to excavate. They might be able to compare dental records while the body or bodies are in the ground, which would give us an answer sooner. We'll have to wait until the forensics team gets here to nail down the timeline. Of course, they'll be coming from different areas of the state, so it depends on their schedules."

"We're sorry." Alex patted Gary's back. "You can call us anytime you need an ear."

"Thanks. I'll probably take you up on it. Right now, I want the truth." He signaled Rain, who stood up and rubbed her head against his leg. "I have a long drive ahead of me. Her owner agreed this would be a good time between construction shifts to do the search, so she lent me Rain. I have to get her back, and it's a three-hour drive. Sheriff, I know you're going to reassign me, and the state will probably be taking over the investigation."

"Probably. Since you're working for me, they won't want me working the case either. But I have friends, and I'll keep you as up-to-date as possible. It shouldn't take too long for identification. Everything we need is on file."

"Right. I'll get out of here." He shook hands with Courtney and Alex, and, after calling Rain's name, he led her back to his SUV. Once he got Rain settled, he went to the driver's side door and waved before getting in and leaving.

"I have to call Honor and Doug to reschedule. We'll have to meet later."

"You won't be meeting anyone here." The sheriff shook his head at her. "Your farm acreage is a crime scene for now. You can leave, and you'll get a call when you can come back."

Courtney frowned. "But we have construction in the house. We won't be outside in the back."

"We'll have to check out the whole house now. I have to call in the forensics team and put the rest of the detective team on alert there may be a case. Could be a while before you're able to get back to work here, depending on what city they're all coming from. We don't have the experts here in the country to dig up bones." He stood by the hole, glancing down at it occasionally, as if the bone they'd discovered would disappear.

"I hope it doesn't take too long." Courtney glanced at Gary. "I wish we knew if it's the Millers, but I don't suppose anyone else is missing."

Sheriff Warren shook his head. "Not your business, but we don't have anyone else missing in this area. Remember, this is all confidential. Not a word to anyone else," he stressed. "So far, we've only found the one bone, but no doubt there'll be more. We have to go through the steps and prove if it's an animal or Gary's parents. The hard part begins after that. Thank goodness he got to borrow Rain. She's the best dog in the state for this type of search. I can't believe she's wrong. Every time in the past, she's been correct about the difference between human and animal remains."

"I've heard cadaver dogs can be wrong if the bones are too old. They think animal bones are human bones." Courtney was beginning to see how long the process to get their construction area back would take. She would plan for a few weeks and hope they'd be able to start sooner. Guilt sprang to life in her gut because she was considering the inn renovation, while Gary had possibly found his parents after all this time. And they weren't alive.

Courtney and Alex left the sheriff in possession of the inn. Alex gave him the key, so he could get inside.

Courtney glanced over her shoulder for a minute as she drove behind Alex to Elm City. Was her inn doomed? Would it get a bad reputation for having a dead body or two in the backyard? She was getting ahead of herself. God knew what He was doing, and she should trust Him.

CHAPTER 5

Later, Courtney stopped at the grocery store and picked up ingredients to make several batches of Bella's Cookies. Her niece had come up with a lot of additions to a basic cookie recipe. People raved about them. St. Mary's Church planned a bake sale for the weekend. She and Alex had all day to bake cookies and invite Honor and Doug to their house on Sunflower Lane to discuss the latest holdup in construction.

They were coming at 3:00 p.m. Plenty of time to start baking and have lunch too.

As soon as they arrived home, they quickly ate their salads, then started baking cookies. The warm, inviting smell of chocolate, vanilla, and cinnamon filled the air as they measured and mixed ingredients for six dozen chocolate-chocolate chip cookies with cinnamon and vanilla chips.

Alex stirred the mixture, his furrowed brow showing his concentration. Once the dough was ready, Courtney scooped spoonfuls of it onto baking sheets and stuck the pans into the preheated oven. The house was already hot, and having the oven on in the kitchen didn't help the situation. She got out some cold lemonade and poured a glass for herself and Alex.

"How is Gary doing?" She broke the troubled silence between them. "It must be tough finding those bones after all these years. I can't imagine."

Alex frowned at the kitchen island. "It's got to be rough. For him, it'll finally bring him closure. He can stop searching and have answers."

"Except someone buried them, so he'll want to find out who killed them before he can totally move on." What if someone killed her parents? Difficult to even fathom. "We can take some cookies to him at the rectory where he's renting. He told me he was happy to be out of the house. Will he want to stay around here or move?"

"Well, he has a job. And he'll at least stay until he finds out what happened to them. I suppose it depends on how well he likes it here, and if he wants to stay around the area where his parents were killed," Alex said.

"We'll have to wait to take him some cookies. He won't be back until late tonight if he has a three-hour trip both ways to return Rain to her owner."

"We'll make extra and take enough for the bake sale at the church and more for him. It won't take away his grief, but it can't hurt."

Alex nodded. "Good idea."

Courtney took a gulp of her lemonade. "I want to know who killed them too. Someone's gotten away with murder for eight years. Someone in this neighborhood. Someone who wanted it to appear like the Millers left the area and went on their way to Virginia."

"It's bothering me too. What if one of our local construction workers is a killer?"

"We agreed to ask questions around here, and we owe Gary. Especially for the price he gave us. Tomorrow's bake sale will be a good place to run into people casually and ask questions." She finished her lemonade and peeked at the cookies in the oven. "Can you find a timer? The one on the stove isn't working."

Alex started rummaging through drawers. "I've been worried about this. I don't want you searching for a murderer." His voice was muffled as he shoved things around in the silverware drawer.

Courtney stilled in front of the oven and stared at him open-mouthed. He had no right to tell her what to do. "You don't have a choice, honey. I'm going to help Gary all I can. We agreed to do this. Remember?"

He groaned. "I didn't realize how dangerous this would turn out to be. I'd hoped his parents got out of town before something happened to them."

Her anger morphed into a giggle. "You didn't sound like yourself just now. You've never ordered me to do or not do something. It was a little weird."

He struggled to pull the timer out of the back of the drawer and held it up in triumph. He handed it to her. "Here."

She took it, checked the cookies, and set the timer for ten minutes. She placed the timer on the yellow counter.

He stepped over and pulled her into a hug, which she didn't resist. "I don't want you to get hurt, so at least promise you'll be careful, whatever you do."

"I'll be careful." She smiled up into his worried eyes and kissed him on the chin. "Very careful."

"Okay."

They stayed together until the timer rang. Courtney reluctantly stepped away, although her shirt was wringing wet with sweat. She pulled the cookies from the oven, set the pans on top of the stove and began working on another pan. They finally finished baking and agreed to wait for Honor and Doug on the back deck where it was cooler.

After a quick shower and a change into another pair of shorts and a sleeveless shirt, she made up a plateful of cookies and more lemonade. She left it all in the fridge and joined Alex on the deck as they waited for Honor and Doug. They planned to ask questions about the activity at the inn.

CHAPTER 6

When Honor and Doug arrived, Alex led them out to the back deck. "It's too hot in the house without decent air conditioning. That window unit isn't a lot of help."

"This late heat wave isn't totally unusual, but not common either," Honor said. "It's about eighty degrees out here."

Courtney stepped outside with a tray holding a plate of cookies, four glasses, and a pitcher of lemonade. "Well, it's about 200 degrees in the house, so this is an improvement." She smiled at her guests.

Doug grabbed a cookie. "So, about the bones they found…anything new? Are they human?" He didn't take a bite until he asked.

Courtney sensed Alex's annoyance by the way he sat up straighter in his folding chair.

How had word gotten out already? The bones were only identified this morning, and the sheriff swore Gary to secrecy. Obviously, there was a leak in the department.

"They've barely started. We had to leave last week before they did any digging and are in the dark as much as everyone else."

Honor frowned. "How about the construction? What are we going to do?"

"We're on hold until they clear the scene," Courtney explained. "No one can go out to the construction site until we get a call from the sheriff." She tried to change the subject. "Anyone want some lemonade?"

After a chorus of yesses, she poured them each a glass.

"We heard there were holes all over the backyard." Doug took a big bite of cookie, spewing a few crumbs onto the boards beneath his chair.

"Who told you?" Courtney demanded.

Doug appeared to have all the information already. Only four people knew about the holes, and none of them would have talked about it. She might need to call the sheriff's office and let him know.

Doug looked at Honor, who shook her head, appearing bewildered. "Don't remember. We called each of the workers to tell them we're on hold for the time being. Maybe one of them?"

"Well, if you do, let us know." Courtney was more concerned than ever one of her hired construction workers dug the holes. "I'll go around and talk to the workers individually and take them their paychecks. Why do you believe someone dug up the backyard?"

"The rumor is for jewels. I doubt if whoever buried the bodies dug the holes. They wouldn't want to disturb the area." Honor took a small bite of cookie. "Yum. Vanilla. We agreed to put sod over the backyard, so we wouldn't have been doing much to the ground already there. They might never have found the bone if someone hadn't dug there."

"Scary." Courtney stared at Honor. "Aren't you afraid? Someone killed them."

Honor nodded slowly. "It's concerning, but nothing's happened for eight years. I guess we've gotten complacent, thinking whatever happened to the Millers happened somewhere else. But I definitely see your point. We'll all have to be careful."

"Someone must have thought it was their last chance to find any buried treasure." Courtney took a sip of her drink. "So, we'll have to wait until something else is discovered. And you're right. Be careful. Let's go over the plans for the inn, so I can think about something else."

She cleared off the picnic table someone placed on the back deck before she and Alex moved into the house. Honor pulled out the folder she'd brought along with her.

With the plans spread out across the table, Honor pointed to one of them. "This is the second floor. We're going with two apartments. Here and here." She tapped her pencil against the paper. "There will be a hallway between the two, so they don't share any walls. That means a separate entrance for each home and maximum privacy."

Courtney nodded in agreement. "These are the two staircases, here and here." She pointed to opposite sides of the floor arrangement. "And an elevator-type lift here." She pointed to another corner of the paper.

"Right," Honor agreed.

"The second-floor plan looks good," Courtney said, sending Alex an inquiring glance.

He nodded. "Our new home with another apartment for guests. Can't wait."

"Okay." Honor pulled two papers from the stack and set them side by side. "The downstairs where the paying guests stay is a little more complicated." She continued with more description of the layout, her eyes bright when she finished. "What do you think?"

Courtney's excitement built throughout their conversation. This was exactly what she and Honor talked about and what she'd dreamed of for the inn. "Perfect." Her voice stuttered at the end, tears ready to fall.

Alex put his arm around her, and she smiled up at him. "Isn't this great?"

He smiled back. "If it makes you smile."

"Oh, you two," Doug mocked.

Courtney shrugged off his words and wiped the moisture from her eyes. "Okay. Let's see the rest of the first-floor plans."

"Good idea," Alex agreed.

Courtney loved how much Alex supported her plan and let her run with her vision of a dream inn.

Honor showed the sketched-out potential layouts for the offices, kitchen, and guests' rooms. "The kitchen will be the first room on the left, and the offices will be in line next. On the opposite side, we'll have the guests' rooms."

Courtney pointed to an area at the end of the hallway. "And this is our sunroom?"

"Exactly. We'll connect it to the deck, which will lead down into the backyard," Honor agreed.

"Where, if you're lucky, you'll find your own archaeological dig." Doug's joke fell flat.

Courtney saw Honor's stony stare at him. "Sorry." He didn't sound sincere.

***

When Honor and Doug left, Courtney asked Alex, "Why is Doug so interested in the Millers' disappearance and the bone in the backyard? Not to mention, he's acting like such a jerk."

"Your guess is as good as mine, but I would definitely start investigating him," Alex told her. "I don't like him."

She grinned at her husband, surprised by his intolerance. It took a lot for Alex to express his dislike verbally. "Are you getting interested in the mystery?"

"Trust me. The faster we solve this, the faster we get to move into the wonderful apartment we saw on the plans. Think about it. Functioning central air. I'm a little concerned about the heat in this place when it gets cold, but I know the apartment won't be ready for us until closer to the end of winter."

Buoyed by seeing the plans and her dream fulfilled, Courtney couldn't stop smiling. "It's going to be fine. We'll be fine. Besides, the community will rally around to find us another place to stay if it becomes necessary."

"There's my half-full-glass girl."

Her smile turned grim. "We've spent so much time and money; I need to keep up my spirits. If this inn doesn't work out because of death and late construction, we'll never make up the costs. We're in too far to back out now. We have to trust God has a plan."

"Maybe it's saving Gary and bringing him back to God," Alex said.

"Maybe." Helping people with their mental health and spiritual journey topped her list of goals for the inn's success. But she didn't need the inn to be of service to others. Despite all the concerns about finishing construction on the inn, people were paramount, and she could do other things if the inn didn't work out.

They needed to turn a corner and find a clue to help Gary solve what happened to his parents. If there were more bones, and they turned out to be Gary's parents, the investigation had taken a big leap. The police would at least have the bodies, and maybe some further evidence.

CHAPTER 7
Wednesday, October 9th

Wednesday morning, Courtney answered the knock on their door. Gary stood there. By his expression, she could tell he had news.

She opened the door. "Good morning."

"Morning. Do you have a few minutes?" He stood there shuffling his feet. "Is Alex home?"

"Yes, I have all day for you, and so does Alex. He's hanging up a load of laundry and will be right back." She realized Gary might be more comfortable with something in his hands. "Come into the kitchen with me."

He followed her, and she reached into a cupboard for a blue mug and handed it to him. "Do you know how to use a Keurig?"

"Yep."

She pointed out the bowl of pods on the counter nearby. "Search for what you'd like and make your own coffee." She smiled at him.

"Feel like I'm back in the military." He let out a strained laugh but relaxed.

"I'll be right back." She hurried to get Alex, more so she could hear Gary's news than because of any need to rush.

Alex glanced up from folding a pair of jeans.

"You almost done?"

He nodded at the two shirts laid out on the bed. She grabbed one of the hangers and stuffed it inside the shirt. "Hurry up. Gary's here with news."

He grabbed the other shirt and hanger, his movements swift and sure. "You left him alone?"

"He needed a moment, so he's making a cup of coffee. Or tea. Or chocolate." They started toward the hallway back to the kitchen.

"Probably doesn't need the caffeine." Alex noticed the shadow ahead of him.

Gary stood in the kitchen doorway, laughing. "You're right. I don't. I took a decaf."

The coffee maker spluttered and was done. He went back and grabbed the cup.

They joined him in the kitchen. "Let's sit at the table." Courtney perched on one of the chairs, and the men joined her.

"They found two bodies and have identified them as my parents." Gary didn't waste time with preliminaries. "I can't believe after all these years, I've finally found them."

Courtney laid a hand on his. "I'm sorry. Must be tough."

He nodded. "I've buried my feelings for a long time. At least I tried. At first I hoped they'd taken off to sightsee while I was in the Air Force. I didn't blame them. They were afraid of what would happen to me. As an only child, they doted on me. And they were excellent parents."

He paused, as if reliving some memory. A range of emotions crossed his face. "I miss them." He stopped there.

Courtney stood up and gave him a quick hug. He fought tears as his eyes turned red.

"Do you want us to give you a few minutes?"

He wiped his eyes with one of the napkins on the table. "No. It's all right. It's good to talk about it, as long as you can deal with some up-and-down feelings being dumped on you."

Alex exchanged a glance with Courtney. "We're all about that. All day, if necessary."

"I hope I won't be a mess for long, but I guess my wish won't be granted. It's going to take a while to come to some kind of acceptance." He took a deep breath, letting it out slowly.

"My biological father died in a car accident when I was a baby, and my mom met my stepfather. They fell in love at first sight and were incredibly happy with each other. He waited until I was eight to adopt me. He wanted me to make my own choice, although he wanted to adopt me from the moment he met my mom.

"I was one of those lucky kids with parents who loved each other and passed on good values and God's love, even if I'm on the fence about what to believe right now. I couldn't ask for more." Taking deeper breaths, he didn't say anything more for a while, just sipped his coffee.

Courtney got up to put a few cookies on a plate to give him time. She prayed for Gary to find assurance in God's love and assumed Alex prayed too as he sat there quietly.

When Courtney set the plate of cookies on the table, Gary cleared his throat. "They were murdered, of course." He stared directly at them.

Courtney was sure most of the community would assume foul play since the bodies had been buried.

"We won't tell anybody anything you say." Alex patted his shoulder. "Of course, the whole neighborhood knows it's murder. Small towns."

Gary shrugged and smiled. "As long as our discussions are secret. I trust the two of you."

Courtney started sniffling.

"Now, don't you start crying," Alex told her. "Then I will too."

"Well, I feel bad for Gary, and I can't do anything for him." She smacked Alex's arm lightly. "Except find the murderer."

Gary's lips pressed together. Whether to stop from crying or laughing, she wasn't sure. "You two! Enough. I sound like a school teacher. No one outside of law enforcement is investigating."

"You're right. Enough," Alex agreed.

Courtney giggled. "Now *you* sound like a school marm. Okay. Sorry, Gary. We don't mean to make light of the situation."

It was his turn to pat her hand before withdrawing his own. "It's what I needed."

"You're too kind. So, why are they saying murder, other than the obvious reason?"

"They were both shot. They've exhumed enough to compare dental records, and they found bullet holes in the bodies. At least they were together at the end." His lip quivered. "I'm glad the tent is still covering the area while they work. I hate the gawkers."

"Shot? Why would someone bury them in the middle of the lawn? Why not somewhere farther out in the country? And why didn't anyone notice the disturbance to the back lawn once the Virginia home sellers reported they never took possession of the house? The sheriff must have been out to the house to at least look around when they didn't show up. Especially when they found the RV in South Dakota." Courtney's sympathy kicked in for Gary. "Are you sure you want to talk about this?"

"Definitely. You two are the only ones I trust. You weren't here when they were, and I doubt if you came from wherever you used to live to do anything other than start a fabulous inn." He threw her a grateful glance and gazed at Alex. "Right?" He raised his eyebrows.

"You got us. We used to live in Chokecherry Valley, and eight years ago…what were we doing, Courtney?"

"Probably in college." She nibbled on one of the chocolate vanilla chip cookies. "I didn't know anything about Elm City. Medora's very touristy, so my friends and I were there a few times. Probably as close as I'd been to Elm City until we started searching properties for sale."

"Me too. I was in jail the past two years and recently got out." Alex watched Gary's reaction.

"I wondered if you'd volunteer that information." Gary reached out his hand to shake Alex's.

After a surprised moment, Alex shook Gary's hand. "I don't keep it a secret, but it rarely comes up in conversation. I'm waiting for the final paperwork for my exoneration."

"Because you didn't embezzle the money." Gary's admiration showed in the approval in his eyes. "You took the fall for the other guy, your friend."

"He was dying of cancer, and I wanted to let him have as much time with his family as possible. Courtney agreed we did the right thing. He took care of me while my parents traveled. He wouldn't have taken me up on the offer if he wasn't too sick to argue. When he died, he left a letter with his attorney admitting his guilt."

"What you did was compassionate. You got your reputation back." Gary took a sip of coffee.

"Yes, but he didn't have to admit it. I already served the full sentence and was home. His family never needed to find out. But he needed to square it with his conscience and God, so he left the letter."

At the mention of God, Gary glanced at Courtney. She stared back with a challenge in her eyes. "Taking care of God's people."

"Okay. If there are more people like the two of you, you might change my mind." Gary set his cup on the table.

Alex sent them each a puzzled glance.

"No one's perfect, so I wouldn't be searching too hard for that," Courtney informed him. "Alex and I certainly aren't perfect. And we may sound noble, but I was furious with him for taking the blame. I felt alone, abandoned, and it wasn't easy living in the community with everyone thinking Alex was guilty of stabbing his friend and mentor in the back."

Gary appeared understanding. "I don't suppose it was easy."

"And Alex didn't have an easy time in prison either. But let's move on to your parents." She'd caught Alex's facial expression out of the corner of her eye. He wanted to change the subject. "Do you plan to have a memorial service for them? We'd be happy to help arrange something for you."

Gary shrugged. "I can't cremate them. A preference for me. The memorial would be a small service by the graveside. A few prayers and anyone who wants to speak. I'm only going to invite a few people. It's a problem, because we don't know who's guilty of their deaths. I'll wait until we have answers. I'll invite you two, Izzy and Finn, and Ed and Elaine and their family. We'll see."

He was ready to discuss something else, so Courtney changed the subject. "You said they're giving out your parents' names to the news outlets tomorrow and asking for help in solving the case. What's the next step for the investigation for us?"

"They finish excavating the remains. They had Rain come back and go through the house and more of the surrounding countryside without finding anything else. As soon as they move everything to the forensics lab, they'll do more testing. In the meantime, the sheriff coordinates with the state in the investigation of my parents' death." He took a cookie and ate a big bite.

Courtney picked up where he left off: "And you keep asking questions at the construction site and elsewhere." Gary would be on site to help with construction when he had time. "I might even ask some questions."

Both men shook their heads as Alex's gaze met hers. "I wish you wouldn't."

"We already talked about this. I'm going to do what I can. We need this to be solved for Gary. He's been in limbo for long enough." Courtney gave Alex a mutinous stare, ignoring Gary.

"I don't agree with Courtney helping either, but we'll both be on site with her." Gary ignored her for the moment and focused on Alex. "I can tell she's got a strong personality and will do this no matter what we say."

"For sure." Alex ground his teeth together.

"I learned." She smirked. "As the oldest girl with two younger sisters, I trained for the role of ordering people around. My older brother was the only one I ever listened to. And my younger brothers hid behind my sisters. But they were all helpful when you were gone for two years." She finished her cookie.

Gary interrupted, "And if we don't solve this, your inn will always be known as the place where the previous owners disappeared and reappeared in the backyard with no explanation. Not good for your business. So, let's work together."

CHAPTER 8
Saturday, October 12th

The hum of laughter and chatter filled the air as Courtney made her way through the St. Mary's Church bake sale, where trays of cookies, pies, and homemade potholders were displayed on the tables. She spotted Gary standing near the back, close to the church. He gazed off into the distance, ignoring the gaiety around him.

"Hey, Gary," she said as she reached him.

His face lit up when he saw her, although his eyes held a note of sadness. "Nice to see you. Where's Alex?"

"He's coming later. He brought our cookie offerings earlier when they were setting up this morning, and now he has some things to do. Did you buy anything yet?"

"No. I've hidden out here by my home. My rented home," he corrected himself.

"When did you move to Elm City?" She believed he'd come as soon as possible to search for his parents.

"As soon as I passed all the criteria to become a deputy a year ago." He looked around to make sure no one was in earshot. "I had the plan set up to declare my parents deceased at seven years—if they didn't show up. I made my plans to coincide with that timeframe to start investigating here. I didn't feel like the sheriff would take me seriously if I wasn't a resident and law enforcement, which played a part. I don't know what's going to happen if I find answers. I'll worry about the consequences when the time comes."

"How did you end up renting the rectory?" She admired the small, well-kept house beside the church. "I'm surprised they let anyone other than a priest or deacon live there."

"I guess being a deputy gave me enough credibility. Plus, I told them it would probably only be for about a year, and they took me up on the offer."

"Does it have decent air conditioning?" She considered their own window unit in the rented home.

"No air conditioning at all, but I'm used to any temperature after the Air Force. I adapt."

She wrinkled her nose at him. "I don't adapt very well. It's irritating me to be so hot day after day. I'm ready for cooler temperatures, hoping the heat works better."

They'd defaulted to the weather for conversation. They couldn't discuss anything personal in front of the people milling around in front of the church. Ears were certainly listening, and a few people glanced in their direction. "Can you come over for a meal tomorrow?"

"Sure. I'm having trouble waiting for more information." He pressed his lips tightly together.

Yelling suddenly erupted on the other side of the yard. She and Gary looked over to see their construction workers, Tyson Collins and Waylon Frederickson, facing each other. Both stood nose-to-nose, glaring.

"I told you to stay away from her," Waylon shouted.

"She hasn't told me," Tyson yelled back.

"Well, I'm telling you."

Tyson's response was too low for Courtney to hear from a distance. Waylon's fist connected with Tyson's jaw, and he fell. She rushed to the area with Gary, but most of the crowd converged on the men, and there was no opening.

All the moms at the bake sale pulled their children farther away from the men. The noisy chaos filled with a chorus of "What happened?" and "Are you alright?"

She finally got a good view of Tyson sitting on the ground, blood running from his nose. He shook his head to reorient himself. Then he peered up at Waylon, who smirked down at him.

"You'll pay for this." Tyson glared at Waylon. "I'm fine," he added to those asking if he was okay. He jumped up and hurried off the grounds, down the street.

"Wow. What was that about?" Courtney quietly asked Gary.

"Tyson's dating Lori," he whispered.

"Who's Lori?" Courtney's gaze searched the grounds for a young woman who appeared interested in Waylon's actions. She didn't see anyone.

"Lori is Waylon's sister. Named after Loretta Lynn, but she refuses to answer to anything except Lori. She's eighteen and graduated from high school last spring. She's not here right now." He must have noticed her staring at everyone.

Courtney recalled Honor or Doug mentioning the same thing yesterday. "Hey, how do you know all this?"

"Research." For a minute his face turned grim.

She guessed he'd checked out all the villagers in his search for his parents. When they bought the house, he told her and Alex he grew up in New York, and his parents moved to Elm City when he joined the Air Force. She could tell he felt guilty they'd ended up in this town and took some of the blame for whatever happened to them. She'd tried to reassure him most people would think New York was a far more dangerous place to live than a small town in North Dakota, but he held on to his guilt.

He'd told her and Alex about his parents' time in Elm City. He didn't visit them because they only lived here for two years. He'd been in the service during that time and didn't have enough leave to visit. The letter to him from his parents informing him they planned to move to Virginia hadn't surprised him. They weren't used to small-town life, so two years was longer than he'd expected them to last in Elm City.

"Tyson seems like a nice guy, although I only spent a little time with him when he helped with the demolition before the structural construction guys came to work on the building," Courtney reached out and caught an empty paper plate the breeze had blown in her direction.

"Waylon considers Tyson too old for Lori. He's twenty-five, and she's eighteen. Maybe because Waylon is forty, and he views his sister as still being a baby, it's hard to see her date," Gary said.

"At that age, it's a bit of a gap but not extreme," Courtney said. "Is there some other problem with Tyson?"

"He likes to drink with Johnny."

"Waylon's brother. He's got a drinking problem, doesn't he?"

Gary nodded. "According to local gossip, Johnny has drunk his way through life since he took his first drink."

"How sad. But it also concerns me with him on a construction site. I'm not sure why Patty recommended him, but Honor's fine with it. I trust her. She wants this inn renovation to be completed in the best way." Courtney was confused by the whole situation. "Everyone keeps assuring me Waylon keeps an eye on him, and everything will be okay."

"Because there's a hint Patty's in love with Waylon. Has been for years."

Courtney's mouth dropped open, awestruck. "You *do* know what's happening in this town."

"Yes." If the frown was any sign, he wasn't happy to be aware of the intimate details of all the neighbors. "You should also know about your other problem on site. Although I don't usually pass on gossip, and this isn't substantiated anywhere I could find…"

***

Courtney stood away from the group of tables on the lawn and waited for Gary to tell her what he'd hinted at. His troubled frown warned her this problem might be bigger than hiring an alcoholic to do electrical work. "Spit it out."

"Robb Bearman and Janine Lang don't get along. He's got a bit of a problem with women on the job, and she's got her own attitude."

"Why isn't he upset about Honor being the forewoman? She ranks higher, and he has to take orders from her." In a way, she wasn't surprised at least one of the guys had a problem with a woman construction worker. In certain ways, most areas had gender and racial inequality, among other issues.

"It's a little more complicated. Honor proved her capabilities and worked construction for years. Her father taught her construction techniques from when she was a girl, and she started the business she has now as soon as she returned from getting a degree. She's also more tolerant of people than Janine."

"Janine seemed a little abrasive when I talked with her. But again, it was only brief discussions during the first round of demolition."

"Well, you'll be getting to know them all a lot better now that the next stage involves your workers being here for a much longer time period." Gary gave her an assessing glance.

Courtney groaned. "Months of construction. Anything else?"

"One more thing on the Janine and Robb situation. He's part Native, and Janine made some crack about it one time. Said something she shouldn't have."

"Great." Courtney moved over to the garbage can and dropped the paper plate into the trash. "Honor already knows, so I hope she has a plan to keep the two apart as much as possible."

Would she make it through the construction phase? An accidental fire, one worker throwing a punch at another, racial tension, and gender discrimination. And the big elephants: bones in the backyard and a jewel hunt.

"One more thing. Some of the guys don't like Janine and Brian taking turns leaving the construction site early to pick up their three kids from school." Gary gave her a sympathetic nod. "That's all for now. You'll get through it. You're strong. You have Alex and Honor helping to keep the peace."

She breathed out a sigh of relief. "You're right. I've got them and you. Thanks for telling me. I'm sure it wasn't easy. I'll have to do some hard praying to God to keep the peace."

He grimaced. "Do you really believe God cares?"

"Definitely." She thought about his comments when they found the one bone in the backyard. "Talk to Alex when you have time. He's better at discussing it than I am. But I will say, I have no doubt God cares about you and your life and what happened to your parents. We don't always get the answers we want. He has a reason for that too. Don't you believe?"

He shrugged. "Haven't decided yet."

Courtney giggled. "Do you even know what the inn Alex and I are building is all about?"

A breeze kicked up as they stood there in the church yard by the tables, scattering a few more empty paper plates. It appeared the sale was winding down, and she saw a lot of bare tables. The few left with any merchandise held mainly non-edible goods, such as potholders and knitted tea cozies. She waited for Gary to answer her question about their inn and what they planned to do with it.

"Of course I know what you're trying to do." He grinned. "I haven't gone senile. You laid it out nicely when you bought the house. The plan is what sold me. The fact you were trying to help others."

"All well and good." Courtney heard the bite in her voice. "But…"

"But you thought because I understood your mission, I believe in your God." His voice was gentle.

"Well…yes." She stumbled over the words. Was Gary meant to be their first mission? Could she help him find his parents' murderer? Could she somehow convince him God existed and to trust Him?

She grinned at him. "We're getting too serious. However, it gave you something else to think about instead of your own problems, didn't it?"

"Definitely." He relaxed at her smile, dropping his arms to his side.

"Want something else to keep busy when you're not deputizing?"

He appeared wary. "Maybe."

"Join us at the construction site when we get back there and restart. If you work, we'll pay you. If you want to wander around looking for clues, go ahead. I'm betting the person who dug those holes is among the construction workers. They all knew we'd be breaking for the weekend before we got going again on Monday."

The thoughtful look in his eyes told her she'd intrigued him. "What a good idea. A hammer in my hands would be a great disguise. It would give me a chance to check out the group of construction workers. Four of them were at my parents' party the last night they were alive: July fourth. Izzy told me."

She considered his point. "I hope it's not one of them, but I'll keep an open mind, along with my eyes."

Gary gazed around the yard. "I'm going to help these people put away the tables and chairs."

The conversation ended, but they'd be spending more time together. Maybe she could work in some God talk with him occasionally. "Sounds like a plan."

They split up and started helping. Alex joined her shortly after she and Gary parted, and the churchyard was soon clear. After Gary declined her invitation to lunch with them, she and Alex made their way to Patty's Diner.

She had no desire to heat up their house again today by cooking. The weather forecast promised temperatures in the sixties for Sunday, and she couldn't wait for the cooler air. She smiled to herself that the weather forecast was of such importance when she had plenty of problems to think about.

CHAPTER 9
Monday, October 14th

Monday arrived, rainy and cooler, with random light showers. Courtney was relieved the heat had been replaced by air she could breathe deeply without suffocating.

Her first order of business was to discuss the construction delay with her workers individually. She called them all yesterday to say she'd be out to their farms to tell them the new plan.

She was taking advantage of the break to investigate the Millers' murders. Going out to everyone's homes on the pretext of updating them and giving them their paychecks was the best way she could think of talking to them. Alex wanted to come with her, but she thought she could find out more if she went by herself.

She started with the Langs. Janine and Brian lived on their farm with their three children, south of Elm City about five miles. The gravel roads were slightly wet, but not enough rain had fallen yet to make them muddy or slick. At least the dust had settled. With her truck window open, she sang along to the song on the radio. The country and western song reminded her of Johnny and Waylon. They were on her list today, and she hoped to meet their sister, Lori, too.

When she turned into the Langs' front yard, she was surprised to see a large two-story house, a silo and red-painted barn, along with numerous small buildings and steel bins. It looked like a large outfit. So why were the Langs working construction on her project? Did all farmers need extra money? Even the bigger operations?

The front door of the farmhouse opened, and Janine stepped out to greet her. Two collies ran up to Courtney and barked as she got out of the truck.

"Don't worry about them," Janine yelled from her position at the front door. "They're harmless."

Both dogs appeared to be smiling, and Courtney took turns rubbing each of their heads. "Good dogs."

Janine joined her, looking fresh in a pair of black shorts and a white-and-black striped t-shirt. Her feet were stuck into a pair of navy sneakers.

While Janine and Brian had three children, she appeared more fresh-faced than expected with her dark fly-away, shoulder-length cut and clear brown eyes. Must be all the clean air. Well, country air. There was the definite smell of animals nearby.

"Let's go inside and talk." Janine walked toward the house with Courtney following. "I've made some blueberry muffins, and the kids left some orange juice."

"Sounds delicious." Courtney loved any pastry items. Blueberry muffins sounded wonderful. Her appetite returned as the heat level lowered. "Where are the kids?"

"They're in grade school now." Janine laughed. "The teachers planned a walk to see the few colorful leaves left on the trees. With the unusual October heat and the wind blowing, they've pretty much dried up and fallen off the trees."

They entered the house directly into a mud room to leave shoes and coats then entered the main area, which featured a kitchen with a large island and a larger living room.

"Let's sit at the island," Janine suggested, chewing on a nail.

"The trees are still pretty in some areas. I find it interesting some trees shed their leaves earlier than others. Your house is gorgeous." Courtney took two checks out of her jean's pocket and set them on the island.

"Thank you. We worked hard on it. Brian and I took advice from Honor, and this is the result. She's good." Janine placed a blueberry muffin on a plate in front of Courtney, where she'd settled on a stool by the island.

"I've brought your paychecks, since we don't know when construction will start up again." Courtney nodded toward them on the island.

"Thank you. How thoughtful of you." Janine slipped the checks into her own pocket.

Soon a knife, fork, and glass of juice joined the muffin by Courtney.

"Do you want butter?" Janine asked, chewing her fingernail and scanning the island.

"No, thank you. I've never picked up the habit of buttering my muffins. Is Brian around?"

She took a bite and almost groaned at the delicious taste of fluffy muffin and blueberries.

"He should be here soon. Oh no, I was going to ask if you'd prefer coffee?" Her voice rose at the end, making it a question.

Courtney smiled, trying to put Janine at ease, and shook her head. "Juice is fine. I might take you up on the coffee when I'm finished."

Janine settled on a stool beside Courtney and turned the chair to face her, the island empty in front of her. "I've eaten already."

Courtney didn't tell her she already had breakfast too.

"From what you said yesterday, the renovation is on hold for now?" Janine's gaze darted around the room.

"Right." She swallowed another bite. She rarely baked, but this country hospitality lifestyle appealed to her. If running the inn allowed any extra time, maybe she'd start baking. "We're waiting for the sheriff's department to decide when we can get back to the site."

She heard the front door open.

"Must be Brian. Go ahead, eat your muffin." Janine got up and left the room.

Courtney took her suggestion and finished the muffin as Brian and Janine came into the room.

"Hi." Brian took the seat next to her, which Janine had vacated. Janine pulled a stool around the island and sat down across from Courtney.

"Hi. Thanks for taking the time out of your busy day to talk to me." Courtney swallowed some of the juice.

Brian shrugged. His tanned arms bulged under the navy t-shirt he wore with his jeans. "We would have been at your place today if things turned out differently, so we're getting bonus time here at the farm. Janine told me you wanted to talk to both of us."

"I'm sure you can always use extra time in some way." Courtney didn't remember telling Janine she wanted to talk to both of them. She'd asked where Brian was.

"Definitely. So, Deputy Lachlan is the Millers' son, right?" Brian saved her from having to bring up the subject she wanted to talk about.

The abrupt question came out of nowhere, surprising her. "Of course. He sold us the house."

"Do you want a muffin, Brian?" Janine interrupted him. Her attempt to stop his questions was futile. He waved her away.

"What is he trying to prove as a deputy?" Brian stared intently at her.

Janine leaned back in her chair, and Courtney caught the audible sigh. So did Brian, as he dropped his gaze as if caught doing something he shouldn't.

She found his sudden withdrawal odd. "I have no idea. I guess he needs a job, and why not law enforcement? We hadn't met before the house sale, and Alex and I certainly didn't know anything about Elm City until we saw the house listed for sale."

"Didn't the real estate agent give you any information on the history of the house?" Brian's gaze returned to her face.

Courtney looked down at her hands clenched around her juice glass before she let go and put them in her lap. Instead of her filling Brian in on the renovation and questioning him about the Millers, he took the opportunity to get information from her. She'd forgotten how everyone in the community wanted to know everything about their neighbors. She would have to rethink her investigation techniques.

"Sure. We knew the Millers had disappeared. The information certainly isn't a secret. The realtor told us they found the RV in a ravine in South Dakota." It was her turn to shrug. "No clue the house would offer up anything interesting when we bought it. You were at the going-away party the evening before they left, right?"

Brian glanced at Janine. "We were. No kids at the time, so we partied it up."

Janine glared at him. "You partied and almost started a fire. Not to mention nearly impaling someone with fireworks."

Brian ducked his head, avoiding his wife's anger. "None of those fireworks went near anybody. Everything turned out okay."

"He decided to stuff about ten different fireworks into the hole all at the same time." Janine's disdain hung in the air. "In the backyard, Simon dug space for one firework at a time, which he carefully made sure pointed toward the sky before he set it on fire. Brian wanted a bigger display."

"And it was wild and crazy. I never saw such a display so close." Brian smiled at the memory.

"Let's say, he was the only one enjoying it, except maybe Doug. The fireworks headed in all directions, and the rest of us ducked for cover."

"Well, it was a quiet night otherwise," Brian defended himself. "That was the real send-off."

"Right." Janine rolled her eyes. "We were also eight years younger at the time. I hope you've gained some sense in the intervening years."

Brian didn't answer.

"Did that end the evening?" Courtney interrupted their marital squabble.

"Pretty much. We stayed about fifteen minutes longer, and then everyone left at the same time," Janine told her.

Courtney couldn't think of anything else to ask them, so she stood to leave. "I stopped by to say we'll start construction again as soon as possible. I appreciate the opportunity to come see your place and drop off your paychecks."

"Would you like a tour?" Brian followed closely behind her down the hallway.

With her hand on the doorknob, she turned to glance back at him. Janine stood behind his tall frame. "Not today, thank you. I have to talk with the other workers." She stepped outside and breathed in the semi-fresh air.

"Well, maybe next time." Brian loomed in the doorway.

"Thanks for the muffin, Janine. I'll be giving you both a call. Hopefully soon." She hurried to her truck, patting each dog on the head one more time before hopping into the cab. Brian watched from the farmhouse doorway. She didn't see Janine behind him, but she waved. He lifted a hand and disappeared into the house.

Courtney drove away, hoping her next two visits would be more fruitful. She drove slowly down the road to visit Robb Bearman.

CHAPTER 10

Courtney pulled to the side of a country road, in plain view of vehicles coming from either direction. She'd planned out her route this morning and knew the way to Robb Bearman's ranch, but she wanted to set up her phone for speaker calling so she could talk to Alex. Once she had everything set up, she dialed Alex and resumed her drive.

He answered on the first ring. "Hi, honey."

"Good morning. How's your day going?" Her breathing resumed a normal rhythm at hearing his voice.

"All calm here. How about you?" he asked.

"Good. I finished talking to Brian and Janine Lang. She fed me a tasty blueberry muffin, and he ruined it by quizzing me about the Millers and Gary," she grumbled. "I was supposed to be asking the questions."

He laughed. "You like your muffins and waffles and pancakes and donuts…"

"Enough." She laughed with him. Life righted itself.

"What did he ask?"

"Why was Gary a deputy? Did we know he was the Millers' son? I forgot how everyone in a small town wants the inside scoop, and apparently we have it right now."

There was a pause. "Interesting. Do you think he had something to do with those bones?"

"Maybe." She almost closed her eyes to block out the image of a skeleton, but driving and closed eyes didn't mix. "Yeah. I hope he's not involved. I like Janine. She was a trifle nervous, or else she always chews her fingernails. And sometimes Brian seemed intimidated by her."

"It would have taken two people to get the RV away from the house. At least I can't think of any other way. One to drive the RV and dump it in the ravine, and a second person to drive another vehicle to take them back to Elm City."

"You don't think they called an Uber?" Courtney smiled at her own joke.

"Funny."

"I did get them to talk about the party the last night at the Millers' house. Apparently, Brian got drunk and nearly started a blaze by setting off too many fireworks at once. According to him, it was no big deal when all the guests ducked for cover." Courtney hated loud noises and wasn't a fan of fireworks.

"Must have been fun." His tone sounded grim.

"Janine said the party ended shortly after, so I'd say it was a show-stopper. That's all I got from them. What are you doing?" She spoke over the sound of the engine and the gravel hitting the side of her truck.

"Talking with Honor. Or, I should say, I talked on the phone with her. She asked when we could get back on the property."

"I'd like to make a recording telling everyone they'll be the first to know after we do. Depending on who is running the gossip mill that day." Courtney rubbed her ear bud to reposition it.

"Right. Well, now I'm going to take a trip to Patty's Diner and see what she has to say. Unless you want me to come to your next appointment with you?" He sounded anxious.

She was tempted. "No. I'll be fine. I'll be at Robb Bearman's next."

"Okay. Take care of yourself and call if you change your mind."

"Will do." She hung up and questioned her judgment. There was nothing to fear. She knew nothing about what happened to the Millers. She and Alex had never met them. Robb was not a suspect, in Gary's view. At least not when she and Alex had discussed investigating for Gary at the house closing.

Did she need to be scared of everyone in the area until the Miller case was solved?

CHAPTER 11

Courtney met Robb when he did the pre-demo with the other construction workers before the structural beams were put in, but she had never been out to his place. Like the Langs' home. She continued thinking about the situation at the inn as she drove along the gravel road to inform Robb of the construction project updates.

As she pulled into the short driveway, the contrast between this farm and the Langs' farmstead stood out starkly. Robb's house was a small one-story square box. It looked like space for only a few rooms. Just the necessities.

There was a barn with peeling paint and no silo attached. A few steel bins and a few outbuildings filled out the rest of the yard. A herd of cattle grazed in the distance. Robb was known for his range cattle more than farming crops, although he did both.

As she pulled the truck up in front of the house, she caught a glimpse of Robb in her rearview mirror. He came striding toward her from the barn. His wiry, slim body hid the power she knew he controlled. The wispy, thin hair also defied his true strength. When they'd done the pre-demo before the structural beams were put in, any doubt of his strength disappeared. In fact, despite Brian's flexing biceps, she figured Robb could beat him in a fight.

She hopped out of the truck, and they shook hands.

"You're right on time." His firm handshake and smiling face put her at ease. He was the quietest man on their construction team, and the one she'd had the least interaction with when he helped with pre-demo. He did his job, spoke little, and left the site.

"Thanks for letting me come out here. I wanted to see where everyone who works for us lives. It's also my way of getting to know the countryside, since we're settling here."

He spread his arms wide. "This is it. We're one of the smallest ranches in the county, but we do okay."

"We?" The question slipped out.

The smile on his face got bigger. "Come. I'll show you." He turned back to the barn, slowing his stride so she could walk beside him.

When they got to the barn, he held the door open for her. They entered a room filled with supplies, and he led her to another door, which opened into a stable-like area. Instead of the horses she'd expected, there were two miniature ponies in two of the stalls. "These are my buddies."

There was a cute black one with white spots, and one completely brown pony. Courtney's heart melted. "Can I pet them?"

"Sure. They love people." He opened their gates, and they edged toward Robb and Courtney.

She patted and scratched their heads. "Wow. What are their names?"

"The black one is Rose, and the brown one is Thorn." He grinned. "Thorn can be a bit mischievous."

"Do they stay inside all the time?"

"No way. They're usually running around, but today the vet is coming for their vaccinations, and I didn't want her to have to deal with muddy ponies," Robb said.

"They're terrific." She was glad she made the trip out to see this softer side of Robb. His care of the horses and his concern for the vet showed a new side to him. He was almost garrulous in comparison to his usual manner.

"They keep me company." He herded each back into its pen, and Courtney followed him outside.

The rain had picked up again, and she had one more stop to make. "Is there an easy way to get to Tyson Collins' place from here?"

"He lives with his parents down the road." He hesitated, opening and closing his mouth again. He wanted to tell her something else.

"Which way?"

"Take a left when you get out of the driveway, and they're about five miles down the road. You can't miss their place. They have the biggest ranch in the area." He didn't sound upset about the difference in their circumstances. In fact, he seemed like a contented man, taking things as they came.

"Thanks. I wanted to tell you, as soon as construction can start again, we'll give you a call. I appreciate you letting me meet your friends."

Her smile must have matched his. "They're cute. I might have to reconsider the 'no animals' rule at the inn."

"Oh, they're fun, but believe me, they can get into trouble. You're welcome to visit anytime and see them."

"Thanks." She shook his hand and opened the truck door. "One more thing." She reached into her jeans' pocket, pulled out Robb's check, and handed it to him. "Here's your paycheck. Since we don't know when construction will begin again, I'm dropping off what we owe and starting fresh when we get going again."

"I appreciate it. There's something I need to tell you." His words stopped her. The smile disappeared from his face for the first time since she'd arrived.

"Sure. What's up?" Was he going to quit? She hoped not.

"Usually, I don't talk about my neighbors, but since you've hired Johnny, I thought I'd let you know. He and Tyson are drinking buddies. Waylon doesn't like the drinking or Tyson. He'd do anything to get his brother sober and doesn't think Tyson is a good influence. A little heads-up." He tapped the hood of her vehicle. "See you soon."

"Bye." She watched him stride up to his house and in the front door. Gary told her Waylon didn't like Tyson dating Lori. Now Robb gave an additional reason for the animosity between Waylon and Tyson.

Realizing she hadn't moved, she opened the truck door, got in, and headed to see Tyson. Interesting. Didn't seem like there was going to be a lack of things going on with the renovation.

She turned left onto the road Robb pointed out on her way to see Tyson Collins. About a mile down the road, there was a big pop, and her truck started swerving. Her heart raced as she tried to bring the vehicle to a stop.

CHAPTER 12

Courtney pulled her pickup to the side of the road and got out to see what happened. The noise came from the back of the vehicle, so she walked on shaky legs to the rear of the truck. She noticed the rear tire on the driver's side was flat.

A flat tire out in the country. Well, she could handle that, and at least the rain had stopped. She pulled down the tailgate and hopped into the back area. She unsecured the spare tire from its position and was about to roll it out of the back when a big red truck parked behind her. For a minute, she was concerned.

Too many mysteries, she told herself as the man got out and walked toward her. *Tyson Collins.*

"It appears you've got a bit of trouble." The twenty-five-year-old smiled at her. His curly black hair ruffled in the wind.

She smiled back. Tyson was charming and knew it. "A flat tire."

"Want me to change it?"

"Sure, but if you're in a hurry, I can do it." She rolled the tire toward him and turned to get the tire iron and jack.

"No. Just coming back in time to meet up with you." He pulled the tire from the tailgate and took the tire iron and jack from her.

Soon, he finished changing the tire and looked like he'd hardly done any work.

If she changed the tire, she'd be dripping sweat and still struggling to remove the nuts and bolts from the flat tire. "Thank you. Any recommendations on the nearest place to get a new tire?"

He hoisted the flat tire into the back of her truck, along with the jack and tire iron. "Try in Medora or Belfield." He leaned back against her truck, his arms across his chest. "You want to talk here, and you won't have to come to the farm? It's only a few miles up the road, so it's up to you. I'm assuming there's not much to say."

She shook her head. "There's not any progress to speak of. The techs are in the backyard now, so we're still on hold until they're finished."

He stared up at the sky. "I'd say we have about a week left before the snow starts. Guessing they want to finish up out there before the weather gets any colder, and the snow covers the ground."

"You're probably right." She watched his expression. "That's the only update. Sorry it isn't more. I didn't have to come out to your place, but I decided it was a good time to get acquainted with the surrounding countryside. I'll stop by your place another time for a tour, if you're willing."

"Sounds good." His arms dropped back to his sides.

"Thanks again for the tire change."

He nodded. "Anytime. It happens in the country more than in town. These gravel roads are hard on tires."

"Alex and I moved from a small town, so we're used to it. Do you plan on sticking around the area to farm and ranch, or are you heading out of Elm City for different opportunities?"

"Oh, I'm committed. I've already got my four-year degrees from Fargo in agriculture and business management. I always planned to return." His gaze lit up.

Courtney was impressed by his assurance. "Good for you. What does the rest of the family think about you staying here?"

"Dad's ecstatic." He grinned. "My two brothers and sister say I'm dumb to stay. Especially my sister. In her eyes, Elm City is a hick town, and she wants the bright lights."

"How old is she?" Courtney was intrigued. Tyson seemed to care about his siblings and was tolerant of their not understanding his decision to stick around.

"Arie is sixteen and knows everything. I sound like a parent. But she's almost ten years younger than me, and sometimes I feel like a second dad." He shrugged wryly.

"Is that why you go out with Johnny? To stay young?" She also wanted to mention the flashy red vehicle parked behind them but kept the observation to herself.

"No. I go to make sure he's okay. I try to get him to stop drinking before he poisons himself. It gives Waylon a break, although he doesn't see it that way." A frown marred his face with wrinkles. "I'm trying to help. Johnny isn't going to stop drinking until he wants to stop."

"You're right." She viewed Tyson in a whole new light. "You're a good friend. I should get going. But first," she reached into her pocket, "here's your paycheck. It covers the time up to when we stopped construction. I'll call you as soon as we're able to get back to the renovation. Thanks again."

"You're welcome." He turned away to go back to his truck.

She got into her own, and he followed her a short distance, until she pulled onto a side road to turn around to get back to town. He pulled ahead of the side road, waving as she went the other way. She waved back before returning to town.

That was helpful. But she hadn't been prepared to quiz him on anything about the Millers after her tire got shredded. Her nerves were too jangled to think straight. There would be ample time to talk to him when they were back renovating the inn.

She had no reason to push a visit on him when they were already talking, and he probably had lots of things to get done on their ranch. She really wanted to get to know the countryside she and Alex were settling in. She'd at least gotten to see the Langs' place and Robb's house and cute miniature ponies. That was a surprise.

***

By the time she got back to the house on Sunflower Lane, her nerves had settled, and she was ready for some warm soup. The chill in the air was fine until she stood outside watching Tyson change the tire. By then, the wind had picked up, and the temperature had dropped.

Alex was home, sitting in front of several spreadsheets covering the kitchen table.

She pecked him on the cheek. "How's my favorite accountant doing?" She sat on a chair beside him.

"Struggling to stay focused." He pushed some of the papers away from him and looked up. "What's going on with you?"

"I visited Robb and the Langs at their houses. Very interesting impressions I got from the Langs. Maybe I imagined the tension between Janine and Brian." She didn't tell Alex about the impression Brian was flexing his biceps to impress her. Maybe she was wrong.

"Did she seem uncomfortable around him?" The concern in his voice made Courtney recall the scene around the table.

"More like she wanted to punch him." She smiled at Alex. "You can relax, but we'll keep an eye out when we're with them. Janine let him steer the conversation. More, I think, because she didn't have anything else she wanted to say than because of some control issue. But who knows." She started to second-guess herself, remembering the nail biting.

Alex patted her hand where it rested on the table. Now he looked concerned about her. "I trust your judgment. We'll see how things go."

"Thanks. You're always so positive. I'm going to make some soup. Do you want some?"

He checked the phone beside him. "Can't believe it's almost noon. Sure. And some crackers and cheese to sprinkle on top."

She stood up. "Like I'd forget the cheese. Oh, I did forget something. Never got out to Tyson's place. I got a flat tire on the way, and he happened to stop by and changed it for me."

Alex leaned forward and frowned. "Just happened to come by?"

She gazed at him from the kitchen counter and grinned. "Yes. He wasn't following me. We agreed to meet at their farm, and he was coming back from somewhere to meet me. I had left Robb's place, which is close to the Collins' farm. I'd parked on the side of the road to get the spare tire out when he pulled in behind me."

Alex settled back slightly. "Okay."

She caught a glimpse of fear in his eyes and went to him. She leaned over and rested her head on top of his, putting her arms around him. It was a little awkward, but he moved forward and returned her hug.

"I'm okay," she said. "There's nothing to worry about. What's bothering you?"

"The Millers. Who killed them, buried them in their backyard, and got away with it for eight years?"

She needed him to calm down because she wanted to investigate. And they promised Gary they would ask questions. Of course, Gary wouldn't want them to go far enough to get in harm's way. "We promised Gary. I doubt we're in danger at the moment."

"At the moment."

"You wanted to go with me today, didn't you?" The more time they spent on Gary's case, the more she realized he wanted to protect her.

"Yes." He stroked her hair.

"Sorry. I've been too busy having fun."

"That's what scares me the most."

She stiffened in his arms and stepped back.

"You aren't taking into consideration someone had no problem killing two people," he said. "Gary knows, and the sheriff knows. Most of the town knows." He looked up at her. "I don't want anything to happen to you."

Seeing the vulnerability in his eyes, she spoke softly. "How about I promise to be careful? If I'm asking probing questions, I'll take you with me."

He sighed. "That's not really feasible because I'm sure you'll have spur-of-the-moment questions, but otherwise, yes. Try and tell me where you're going to be, although we've always gone wherever we wanted, and we don't need to keep track of each other."

"How about we put one of those tracking apps on our phones? Would it make you feel better?" Courtney asked. "I don't want to give up on helping Gary if we can."

"I don't want to stop either. We might make some headway helping bring him closer to God. If we can solve his parents' murder, that might help somewhat. We'll have to see."

"Okay. Come help me with the soup and other things. It'll keep you occupied."

He snickered. "Right." He got up and followed her back to the counter. The kitchen was a small square. With the table and chairs taking up most of the room, they were barely able to both maneuver around the counter space.

"I'll be okay." She pulled some things out of the cupboard while he took the cheese and butter out of the fridge. "I've been thinking… What are the chances one of our construction workers was involved? Tyson was only seventeen at the time. He couldn't have pulled it off and kept it quiet.

"Waylon and Johnny were in their early thirties. Janine, Brian, Honor, and Doug were all in their upper twenties, since they're in their mid-thirties now. I can't tell how old Robb is. I'm guessing he's in his lower sixties. Which covers everyone I can think of off the top of my head.

"That means anyone could have done it, except Tyson. They were all in the right age group. They're all suspects. We have to look at the motive for the murder. Otherwise, the whole town could be guilty.

"And why would they believe we know anything? I didn't bring up the bone Rain found. They asked the questions, and I said I had no idea. Plus, we weren't living here until a short time ago."

"Who asked the questions?" he spoke sharply.

"Mainly Brian, but he and Janine were at the Millers' Fourth of July party, so it could be merely curiosity. Robb didn't bring up anything about them, but he had something else interesting to say on another subject." She told Alex about Robb's comment on Tyson's relationship with Johnny and Waylon.

"I guess we'll have to try to keep them in different sections of the project when we can," Alex agreed. "Honor should be aware of this already. Maybe she didn't want to say anything about it."

"Well, she should have." Courtney stirred the tomato soup on the stove. "Should we make grilled cheese to go with this?"

"No. I'm going to have buttered bread and drop the shredded cheese in the soup. But go ahead if you want it."

"No. This is fine." She stirred some more. "Robb had these two cute miniature ponies. He named them Rose and Thorn."

Alex stopped dumping the shredded cheese into a bowl. "Rose and Thorn?"

"Well, I guess Rose is the sweet one, and Thorn gets them into trouble. According to Robb, anyway."

Alex laughed and returned to his task.

"I told him maybe we needed to get a pet or two for the inn," she teased him.

He must have caught the amusement in her voice because he pushed the cheese bowl aside and pulled the bread toward him. "Right. Liability insurance nightmare."

"Exactly," she said wistfully.

Once everything was on the table, they said the meal prayer and dug into the food.

"Did Tyson have anything to say?" Alex's earlier tension seemed to have disappeared.

"No, but he did tell me we'd need to take the tire to Medora or Belfield to get it fixed." She took a bite of her bread, relaxing back against her own chair. How long would it be until they had an answer from the sheriff about the renovation schedule?

CHAPTER 13
Monday, October 24th

Construction was delayed for two weeks before they were allowed to continue. On the first day they could get started again, Alex and Courtney arrived at the site early in the morning, but Honor's vehicle was already parked in the yard when they got to the inn.

She came out of the building to meet them. "Finally. I thought the police would never let us back in. Now we can start. I've got the first jobs sorted for the crew. Robb and Tyson are jackhammering any concrete where Waylon needs to add plumbing in all the guest rooms.

"Janine and Brian are demolishing everything in the corner kitchenette area and along the rest of the wall for the television room. Johnny is studying plans for the kitchenette wiring and the public restroom on the opposite side of the room. He'll probably start in the kitchenette area. Waylon can start on the other side where the restroom plumbing goes. They've already gutted the area because there was nothing structural there."

Courtney shook her head. "Johnny's thorough. He's been planning for the past two weeks while we waited. I'd say he's ready."

"Which is great," Honor said enthusiastically. "He wants to get it right. You're lucky he's into this renovation. He's the best at what he does. Waylon's influence will keep him on task."

"And the drinking?" Courtney couldn't hide her worry.

"He waits until he leaves work, and Waylon never lets him come to the site in the morning if he's drunk. You get fewer days of work out of him, but it doesn't matter, because he's incredibly efficient and does great work. It evens out. We only pay him for the days he shows up," Honor assured her.

Honor clearly had worked with Waylon and Johnny before. If she approved of the situation, Courtney believed in her.

"Okay." Courtney pushed aside her reservations. She'd been trying for weeks. Ever since she found out about the last owners from Gary. Trust God. He would take care of them.

Honor kept Tyson and Johnny in separate work areas. She knew what she was doing. Which was why Alex and Courtney hired her. Recommendations on her work were great, and she could manage the site.

She looked at Courtney and Alex. "So, what's your preference? Knocking down the rest of the unnecessary walls since the structural beams are in place? Or helping Doug and myself with the temporary ramp from the backyard into the house?"

"Do you have a preference?" she asked Alex and Honor.

"I don't," Alex said.

Knocking down walls appealed to her and her nerves, but she'd be more productive helping with the ramp. Plus, she might discover why Doug asked so many questions about the Millers, and she could ask him about the jewels. "The ramp."

She nodded at Courtney. "You okay with demolishing walls?" Honor asked Alex.

His smile grew. "Sure. I look forward to it."

"Great. Wait here for a few minutes, and I'll be back to work with you. Come on, Courtney."

They walked to the back door and opened it. Doug had lumber, nails, and other construction tools to help build a wide ramp. He wiped his forehead with a bandana he wrapped around his neck. "You ready to help me?" he asked, staring at Honor.

"I'm trading with Courtney. She's going to help you. I'm going to show Alex how to knock down walls."

"Oh, great," he muttered. He gazed up at them standing above him on the landing. "Glad to have some help. You can either jump down here or go around the building."

To Courtney, it sounded like a challenge. She took it and jumped down. Her left knee protested slightly, but she ignored the twinge of pain. "What do you want me to do, Boss?"

His bad mood wasn't going to affect her. They were all finally working on her dream inn.

When Honor closed the back door without another word, Courtney almost laughed. Honor must have had enough of her husband's surliness for the day. Her attention was quickly taken by

Doug's orders on how to build a ramp. She'd have to work in discreetly asking him questions about the Millers.

CHAPTER 14

For the first ten minutes, Courtney simply followed Doug's instructions. Whatever his view about her when she first started helping him, his mood mellowed the longer they worked together.

"How long will it take to build this ramp?" she asked.

"About two more hours. It must hold up until we get the inside area by the back door done. Then we can use the front door for the rest of the winter. If we get a lot of snow, we don't want to clear snow in the front and back. Adds too much time and work to the project."

"I see." It made sense to her to finish the back area first. She assumed Honor would be directing construction in there soon. Maybe she and Alex were demolishing the back area even now. "So, what do you think about the Millers' bodies being found back here?"

He stopped pounding in a two-by-four that was part of the ramp support. "I can't believe they've been here all this time." He shook his head, appearing confused.

"Why didn't the police find them eight years ago when they first disappeared? Didn't they search the area?"

"They sure did." He leaned against the long handle of the mallet he'd been using to pound the board into the ground. "Obviously, since they were buried, there was nothing to see. And as soon as the RV was found in South Dakota, they started looking in that direction."

He started pounding again then rested a level on the board and another one near it. A few more whacks, and he checked again.

"Appears even." Courtney stood there, unsure what to do next.

"Yep. All level."

"So, no one brought in a cadaver dog until Gary did?" she continued.

"Nope. No reason if the bodies were in South Dakota." He stared at her. "You seem mighty interested."

She flushed but nodded. "Well, they were found right there." She pointed to a spot in the backyard where obvious digging had left a huge dip in the middle of the landscape.

"Right. Wish someone would have taken care of all those holes before we started today, but that's not the sheriff's job, and we weren't allowed on the site until today. We'll have to fill in all the holes so no one gets hurt." Doug shrugged. "Do you want to hear something interesting about the big hole?"

He had her full attention. "Definitely."

"That's the spot in the yard where Simon shot off the fireworks. And then Brian did his stupid stunt, and the evening ended."

Courtney shivered. "Someone made the hole Simon started bigger to bury both of the Millers? Crazy."

"Exactly. I can't wait until the truckload of dirt is brought in, and all those holes are filled. It's creepy back here." His furtive glance held a note of fear before he turned back to building the ramp.

"For sure." Courtney was surprised Doug agreed.

He pulled out another two-by-four and started pounding it into another hole he'd drilled with an auger before she'd joined him. He obviously wanted to get done with the job and out of the backyard. "I'll put in these two other supports, and then you can help me nail in the flooring of the ramp."

"Sure. Who else was at the party?"

He picked up another two-by-four and wrestled it into the last hole. "Just Izzy, Finn, Honor, myself, Janine and Brian. And, of course, Valerie and Simon."

"What about the jewels? Who knows where they are?" Courtney asked, watching him struggle. He wouldn't want to ask for her help with the last board.

He stopped and picked up the mallet. "No doubt the killer has them. They're long gone." He took a big whack at the board and missed.

She picked a piece of dirt off her jeans, pretending not to see. "But everyone seems to think they haven't been found yet."

"Gossip." He took a careful swing and made contact the second time. "The jewels are gone."

"Did you ever see them?" She was getting on his nerves, and this would be her last question.

"Just the one necklace Honor took a picture of and showed me." He started pounding at a steady pace.

Why didn't he want to talk about it? He was the one to bring up the subject when he and Honor stopped by to see Alex and herself a few weeks ago.

Someone figured the jewels were hidden out there somewhere. Otherwise, there wouldn't be holes dug all over the backyard. Which was odd. People kept expensive items in bank deposit boxes and safes. Not a hole in the ground.

Who would suspect the jewelry was hidden in the backyard? Only someone who had spoken to Valerie and Simon. The person who'd caused their death.

Why had they waited eight years to search?

CHAPTER 15

When Courtney and Alex returned home at the end of the day, they collapsed on the run-down yellow-brown couch.

"I'm tired out," Courtney said to her husband, reaching for his hand. "I should have gotten in the shower before sitting down. Standing up will be painful."

He laughed. "I never believed I'd like this kind of work, but it's cathartic to knock things down—despite the blisters."

"Thank goodness I read a lot, or I'd have to get a dictionary." She sighed and settled back on the couch. She turned his hand over and peered at the raised spots. "You'll need to get some gloves."

"I will. Demolishing walls released a lot of pent-up feelings I assumed I'd already purged. Very cathartic."

She laughed, as he expected, at the repetition. He'd done it on purpose to relax her. "We've got a long way to go, so if you have any other experiences you need to cathart, you'll have plenty of opportunity."

"That's not a word," he argued as he pulled her up by the arm. "Let's go get cleaned up. I'm starving."

She realized her stomach was giving off hunger pangs too. "We're going to have to pre-make meals because, I can tell you right now, getting a meal together after a day like today is going to take my last ounce of energy."

"Same here. We've got leftover soup, and I'll make the grilled cheese. Tomorrow we can pick up a pizza from the bar. I hear they're good. We'll have time to get some groceries and plan better."

After they cleaned up and ate, they settled back on the couch together.

"Learn anything new today?" she asked him. "Besides discovering your love of knocking things down?"

"Funny." He gazed up at the ceiling from his slouched position. "Everyone was on their best behavior. Didn't see any hostility or anything like that. Let's see how the week progresses. Right now, everyone's glad to be back at work and relieved we didn't cancel the renovation and leave town."

She snuggled up to him, holding the remote in one hand, prepared to turn on the television and zone out to some mindless show.

"What did you find out from Doug?"

She squeaked her surprise and moved forward to stare at him. "How did you know?"

"Of course you'd be quizzing our workers. Your curiosity isn't going to be satisfied until you find out what happened to the Millers."

"And that doesn't bother you?"

"I married you for better or worse, curiosity and all." He smirked.

"Funny," she repeated his word before settling back against him. The comfort of his warm presence settled her mind. "I want to know what happened. And I want Gary to get answers about what happened. If I can help him, I will."

"It's not exactly without risk." He pulled her closer into a tight hug. "I don't want anything to happen to you. Any of our workers could be involved."

"Maybe, but it's too late. I've already started asking questions. Doug said there aren't any jewels to be found. They're long gone, according to him. They exist because Gary told us, or the Millers wouldn't have been killed."

"They might have died for some reason other than theft. Wouldn't it be easier to steal the jewels some other night, rather than kill them?"

She mulled over the idea while he took the remote from her hand and turned on the television. She watched him flicking through channels. He was done with the conversation, but she wasn't done thinking about it. Or asking questions.

***

The first three days of the renovation passed uneventfully, and Courtney was getting into the rhythm of getting up, going to work and coming home exhausted. Her body definitely wasn't used to the level of physical activity it had gone through.

Wednesday night, she fell asleep the moment her head hit the pillow. She woke from a deep sleep, lying on the bed, wondering what jerked her awake. She groaned at her sore muscles. Then the sound of banging on the front door and someone shouting brought her to her feet.

She jabbed Alex. "Wake up!"

He turned over and sat up. "What's that pounding?"

"Someone's at the front door."

He jumped out of bed, and she shrugged into her flannel robe and followed him down the stairs. The pounding continued, and she could make out the words, "Open up. It's Johnny."

Alex opened the door, and Johnny tumbled into the room.

"He's dead. I can't wake him up." Johnny burst into tears.

Then she noticed the blood on the front of his shirt.

CHAPTER 16
Thursday, October 27th

Alex tugged Johnny into the living room and guided him into the recliner. "Can you get a blanket out of the closet?" Alex asked Courtney. "He's shivering."

As she got the blanket, the question ready to tumble from her lips stayed unspoken. She unfolded the thick navy cotton blanket and placed it over Johnny. The smell of vomit and alcohol made her back up quickly.

He continued to mumble, "He's dead."

Alex got down on his knees beside the chair. "Who's dead, Johnny?"

"Waylon. He's bleeding, and I can't get him to wake up." His slurred words were even harder to understand as his sobs increased.

"I need to go check on him," Alex told Courtney. "You stay here with Johnny, and I'll be back as soon as I can."

"I can go with you." She didn't want Alex to go alone.

"You stay here with him. He's not sober, so who knows what I'll find."

The blood told Courtney something was wrong. Had Waylon fallen and bumped his head, or did he have some other accident? "You're right. Hurry up. Maybe he's not…" She didn't finish her sentence in case Johnny's tears started again.

Alex raced to the bedroom and was back in record time. Dressed in jeans, a sweatshirt, and cell phone in hand, he nodded to her. "I'll text you as soon as I have information."

She sat down on the couch across from Johnny, who seemed to have fallen into a stupor.

Every once in a while, he whispered, "What am I going to do without him?"

Remembering her phone in the bedroom, she glanced at him. He wouldn't notice her being gone for a minute. She got up to get her phone.

Johnny looked up suddenly. "Don't leave me."

She placed her hand on his arm. "Just for a moment. I need to get my phone so Alex can call us. I'll be right back."

He nodded, tears bright in his eyes.

She hurried to get her phone and was back within a minute, glancing at the screen to see if there was any word from Alex. Of course there wasn't anything yet. Although Waylon lived only a few houses down from them on their street, Alex would need time to get there and take a look. Check to see if Waylon was hurt instead of dead. She prayed he was alive.

The on-duty police could be anywhere in the county. A drawback of living in a small town. If they needed to come, it could take a while depending on their location. But Gary was a deputy and lived close, in the rectory. He could be there in five minutes, if he wasn't on duty elsewhere.

She sent a text explaining what Johnny said about Waylon and there was blood on Johnny's shirt. She added that Alex was checking Waylon's house, and she was in the living room with Johnny but didn't want to speak in front of him.

Her phone pinged with a text from Gary: "On my way. I'll call an ambulance in case it's needed."

Her phone rang. Alex. "Hi."

"He's dead," Alex told her. "I think he's been shot or stabbed. There's blood in the chest area. Kind of smeared, which could be from Johnny trying to see if he was alive. I sure hope Johnny didn't do this. I don't see a weapon anywhere, so I'm guessing murder."

Courtney shivered. "Be careful. What if whoever did it is still around?"

"I doubt it, but I'll be careful."

"Please." She couldn't speak freely in front of Johnny, and he wasn't letting her out of his sight.

"I promise."

Hearing him say the words brought lightheadedness. "Thank goodness I texted Gary to meet you there."

"You did?" Alex sounded relieved.

"Certainly. And I'm glad I did. He should be there soon."

"Okay. I'll be here waiting. You doing okay with Johnny?"

She watched him. He appeared to be dozing but was probably aware of what was happening. "Fine." He'd know what she meant. Their code for "as good as could be under the circumstances."

"Hopefully, once Gary gets here, I can leave. We're probably up for the night, though, because I'm sure he'll bring in the sheriff."

She knew what that meant too. Make some coffee. "Talk to you as soon as you're able to call."

"Thanks. I'm sending Patty over there. She's the twins' closest friend." He hung up.

When she put her phone in the pocket of her robe, Johnny stared at her. His sad eyes made her want to cry. "He's dead, isn't he?"

"I'm afraid so," she said gently. "I'm sorry."

He nodded, seeming to have been absorbing the news since he arrived. "I should go back there."

"No," she said sharply.

He sat up quickly. "Why not?"

"Sorry. I didn't mean to be abrupt. Alex is handling things with the ambulance and the police. He'll tell us when there's something you can do. You don't want to go back now. Patty's coming to keep us company."

"Okay. As long as Alex is there. He'll take care of W-waylon," he stuttered his brother's name.

"Would you like some coffee? I'm going to have some. It'll be a long night. Or if you want to lean back and close your eyes, go ahead."

"I'll take coffee." He appeared more alert already as she walked into the kitchen to get two cups of coffee. She made his plain black and a raspberry-flavored pod for her cup. She needed a little comfort.

Maybe after Johnny had a cup of coffee or two, she could ask some of the questions swirling around in her brain. Did he know what happened to Waylon? Why was he at Waylon's so late after a night of drinking? Or had he been drinking at Waylon's house? Doubtful. She imagined Waylon didn't have any booze in his house.

Her cell pinged. Pulling it out of her pocket, she glanced at the display. Alex texted, "Gary's arrived."

She texted back, "Glad you're not alone there anymore."

She relaxed slightly. Now it was a matter of sitting on the couch until there was additional news. She hoped Johnny would fall asleep. Between the drinking he'd done and finding Waylon, he appeared exhausted.

What she wanted to do was join Alex. Not to see Waylon's body, but to see what was happening. She sipped her coffee and waited for the next text or for Alex to return.

Patty arrived about five minutes later. After a brief hug and hello for Johnny, she settled on the couch with Courtney. "Do you want to talk about it?" she asked Johnny.

He shook his head. "I can't believe it. I went there because he called me and said he needed to tell me something. When I got there, he was dead." Silence followed.

Patty didn't break it, and Courtney followed her lead. Patty knew him and the best way to treat the situation better than she did.

"He told me a few weeks ago he wondered who could be searching for the Millers' jewelry. I figured it was related to that. It's all everyone is talking about right now. Whatever he was going to tell me is going to stay a secret, because I haven't got a clue."

Patty coughed. "Would he tell anyone else?"

Courtney found the conversation fascinating. Patty and Johnny might have more information about the Millers' case than they'd shared.

Johnny shook his head and reached up to rub his skull. "I've got such a headache, and I'm dizzy."

Neither woman suggested it had to do with his drinking.

"I'll get you something for the pain." Courtney stood up and went to the kitchen for some pain relievers and a glass of water. When she returned to the living room, she sensed the silence had taken on new meaning. She wasn't sure why. Neither said anything while she was in the kitchen. She would have heard their voices.

"Here." She handed the water and pills to Johnny. "Either of you want more coffee or water?"

"I'll take some coffee," Patty said. "Black. I have to work today."

"Nothing else for me. I'm a little queasy." Johnny's face paled.

"Restroom is at the end of the hall, if either of you needs it." Courtney stepped back to the kitchen doorway. "I'll get you some coffee, Patty."

While in the kitchen, she decided it was time to quiz her guests. If they knew what was going on, it was time for it to come out into the open. Gary deserved closure about his parents, and now Waylon was dead.

She went back to the living room and handed Patty her coffee, sitting next to her on the couch. "What's going on? You two have information about the Millers the rest of the town doesn't have."

They glanced at each other again. Johnny's gaze found his lap, and Patty stared at Courtney. "I don't think we know more than anyone else around here."

"Well, Waylon did. Maybe it's rude of me to say this, but I don't want either of you to find yourself in the same position."

"But he didn't tell me anything," Johnny wailed. "I was too late. I'd been drinking. I thought he could wait. Don't you think I feel bad enough? If I had quit drinking when he texted, he might be alive."

Patty went over to him. Sitting on the recliner's arm, she put her arm around his shoulders. "Don't blame yourself. He could have told us sooner. Whatever he was going to say was a secret he kept, but he might have had evidence for a while. He'd been acting distant the last week. Actually longer. Ever since they found the Millers' bodies. I should have pressed him."

"I didn't notice." Johnny's face fell slack. "I didn't notice." He sagged back against the recliner.

Patty removed her arm and stood up. She took a look at Johnny and made some decision. "Don't blame yourself. Waylon kept things bottled up inside. It wasn't good for him, and in this case, it was fatal. It's not your fault."

She walked back to the couch and sat down. "Let's get some rest. You lean back and close your eyes. I will too. We have a long day ahead of us as soon as the police show up here." She glanced at Courtney. "Things will start happening now."

Courtney's mind went into overdrive. She shouldn't have any more questions, but she did. "You know something. Something big."

"I'm pretty sure this is murder, and Waylon's death will bring new information to the police," Patty said, gazing at Johnny.

"He didn't commit suicide, did he? You said he was distracted lately." Courtney recalled Alex hadn't seen a weapon.

"Not likely." Patty pressed her lips together.

"No way would he leave me," Johnny said, huddling under the blanket.

Whatever Patty knew, she kept it to herself. Courtney wanted answers, but how could she get Patty to speak? She suspected it was best to wait for the police to question her.

CHAPTER 17

Alex had left the house around midnight. He returned at 1:00 a.m. Johnny had fallen asleep and lay snoring on the recliner. He didn't move when the front door opened.

Patty looked up from her second cup of coffee, waved, and mouthed a hello. While Courtney hurried to the door, her finger to her lips, Alex waved back at Patty.

Courtney led Alex back to their bedroom. When they were both inside, she quietly closed the door. "What's happening?"

His face was drawn, his lips pressed together, his eyes red. "Someone did kill him."

She shook her head to remove the image. "Any idea who?"

"Johnny is a suspect, having found him. I wasn't part of any conversation about other suspects they're considering. They asked me about fights at work, and since there haven't been any, the conversation ended. The sheriff told me to leave."

She recalled the argument between Tyson and Waylon at the bake sale. That was weeks ago now. Gary witnessed the fight too, so he could report it. "Why were you there so long?"

"The sheriff was on the far side of the county, and it took him forever to get there. We waited for a doctor to confirm death. He was obviously gone. They asked me a few questions about Johnny, but I couldn't tell them much. Besides, they'll see the blood on Johnny when they come to get him. They're taking him with them to tell his parents and his sister the news."

Courtney closed her eyes. How she'd feared getting a visit like that when Alex was in prison. He hadn't even committed the crime he was accused of but pled guilty to help a friend. Very few people understood how Alex could have spent two years in jail for a crime he didn't commit. They didn't understand Alex's loyalty to his friends. He felt he owed the man who was guilty, and he was paying him back the only way he could.

"Anything else happen while you were there?" she asked him.

"Someone said Waylon might know about the jewels, but the sheriff said it looked more like a grudge killing than a robbery. Nothing else was taken. And let me tell you, our house may be on the same block as Waylon's, but the similarity ends there. He has high-end appliances, electronics, and furniture. It's obvious he's not hurting for money."

"Which doesn't mean much. Plumbers make a lot, and what else is he going to spend it on here in Elm City?" Courtney asked.

"Well, let's go wake Johnny before the sheriff gets here."

When they returned to the living room, Johnny was sitting up in the recliner. He sipped at the cold coffee he'd ignored when Courtney gave it to him hours ago. "What time is it?"

"About 1:30."

"Did I…really see…" He stared down at the coffee, which brought his gaze to his sleeve. There was some blood there. "Guess I did." He shook his head and sighed. "I can't imagine telling Mom, Dad and Lori."

"You'll have some company," Alex told him.

Johnny's face brightened slightly. "You'll come with me?"

"If the sheriff will let me go. If he does, I'll come."

"The sheriff will take me, won't he?" Johnny asked.

Courtney wasn't sure if he meant to jail or out to the farm to tell the family. She hoped they wouldn't arrest him, because she didn't believe Johnny was guilty. He'd been too shaken when he appeared at their door. "Why didn't you call the police right away instead of coming to our house?"

"I saw Waylon." He winced. "Then I ran outside to be sick. I didn't want to go back inside and see him that way, so I ran here." His laugh held no humor. He set the empty cup on the side table.

"Would you like some more coffee? Warmer this time?" Courtney asked.

"No, I'm fine. Except…" His face turned red.

"Restroom is down at the end of the hall," Alex repeated what Courtney told Johnny earlier.

"Thanks." He got up, holding on to the arms of the recliner like an old man. He shuffled down the hallway.

Someone knocked, and Alex opened the door. The sheriff came in with Gary and gazed at the group sitting in the living room. Since everyone knew each other, no introductions were necessary.

"Where's Johnny?" he asked.

"He'll be right back," Alex told him.

Then Johnny came down the hallway, a straight line from the door where they stood. He came to a halt a few feet from them.

Four sets of eyes in his direction might be a bit much, so Courtney lowered her gaze to the floor and stepped back. Alex followed her, and they sat on the couch by Patty.

The sheriff's gaze sized up Johnny. "I'm sorry about your brother. He was a good man."

"Thank you. I'm sorry about your parents," Johnny said to Gary.

"Thank you," Gary responded.

Sheriff Warren said, "I need to talk to Johnny."

Johnny's forehead creased, and his eyes opened wide. "I didn't have anything to do with what happened to Waylon." He plopped down on the recliner as if his legs wouldn't hold him.

"I'm not saying you did." The sheriff stood in front of the recliner, watching Johnny. "I need to ask you some questions about when you arrived at your brother's house."

"It was close to the time I came here. I didn't look at my phone to check the time. Ask Tyson. He dropped me off and left. Didn't even get out of his shiny bright red pickup."

Courtney sensed a hint of envy behind the words.

"So, Tyson should know?"

"He would. Yes." Johnny seemed sure.

"And after you saw your brother, how long did it take for you to get here?" The sheriff pulled out a small notebook and was writing down Johnny's answers.

"Not long. I don't think." He sat brooding for a few minutes. "I was in shock. I tried to revive him. I went over and shook him to wake him up." He shuddered out a breath. "But he didn't move. Just flopped back on the couch.

That's when I noticed the blood, and I was too late to save him. If I had stopped drinking when Waylon texted, and Tyson told me last beer, maybe I would have been there in time to stop whoever did it. Instead, I had to have one more drink."

"So, would you say you were there five minutes? Ten minutes? Longer?"

"Probably between five and ten minutes. It's hard to judge how much time passed while I stood there, willing him back to life."

"Then what happened?"

"Alex and Courtney live on this block, and I knew they would help me. I ran here." Johnny leaned back, spent.

"Why didn't you go to one of the neighbors next door to Waylon?" The sheriff's piercing gaze measured Johnny's response.

"They don't like me," he said simply. "Guess I've caused too much trouble through the years. I figured Alex and Courtney would be more sympathetic."

The sheriff nodded. How often he had been called to one of those neighbors' houses for a fight between Johnny and a homeowner?

"And how long were you with Tyson tonight?"

"He picked me up around nine. I got home around eight from work, ate, and then he came." He started sniffling and reached for the box of tissues on the end table beside the recliner. "What happens next? We need to tell my parents and Lori."

"We'll go out to see them now and tell them." The sheriff closed his notebook and stuck it in his pocket.

Alex said, "Oh, by the way, half the neighborhood's lights have been on since Johnny pounded on our door. I ignored their questions."

"We need to tell my parents and Lori before someone else does," Johnny said, his tone urgent. "Can you drop me at my house to get my vehicle?"

"Not sure how sober you are yet," the sheriff responded politely. "So, I'll drive, and Gary can come with us. Any objections?"

"No, except, can Alex come with us?"

"Not sure that's necessary," Sheriff Warren objected.

"He calms me, and I want him to come. He'd be good with Lori. She's only eighteen." Tears filled his eyes. "Waylon was her favorite. This is going to be hard for her."

The sheriff looked at Alex, his brows raised. "How about it?"

Courtney sensed the fatigue weighing down her husband, but the others wouldn't realize from his manner.

"If Johnny needs me, I'll come along," Alex said.

"Would you mind driving my truck to my parents' house? I need to have my vehicle to return home in the morning."

"Not if the sheriff doesn't mind." He glanced at Sheriff Warren.

"I should also change clothes. I can't go with my brother's blood on me," Johnny said.

"You can change. Deputy Lachlan will take the clothes from you and bag them. As far as Alex taking your vehicle out to the farm, give him the keys to your truck once you're at your place, and I trust him to hold them until you're sober enough to drive," the sheriff told Johnny.

"Let's go. My house is a few blocks over," he told Alex.

After Alex kissed Courtney, he whispered for her to go to bed as soon as Patty left. The others moved toward the door.

Gary held the front door while Johnny exited, with Alex following, and the sheriff brought up the rear. Courtney watched them go with foreboding. They were treating Johnny well enough, but she sensed an undercurrent. Would they do the notification to his family and arrest Johnny after?

Patty was quiet while the sheriff and Gary were there. Courtney studied her after the men left. "What do you think?"

"I'm afraid for Johnny." Patty frowned. "I hope they look around for someone else and don't settle on him because he found his brother. First of all, there's no way Johnny killed his brother. Those two have gone through a lot together."

"Not even if he got angry with him?"

"Not even then. They give each other the silent treatment. I've never seen them throw a punch at each other in all these years."

"I agree with you about Johnny's innocence."

"Does Waylon's death have anything to do with the Millers' deaths?" Courtney's mind was tired but racing through lots of scenarios. Had Waylon figured out who killed the couple? Did he come across something? What was he going to tell Johnny? He would have known Johnny's condition at that time of night wouldn't be great. What would he deem so important, he had to tell Johnny when he wasn't sober?

"It's more than likely the deaths are connected," Patty agreed. "Which means Johnny's innocent."

"I actually considered calling my brother in Bismarck to defend him." Courtney plucked her phone out of her robe. 2:00 a.m. She was so tired.

Patty's brows lifted. "You did?"

"Yep."

Patty smiled at her. "Good. We're on the same page. Hopefully the sheriff finds the guilty party before it's necessary."

"Right. And the second thing?" Courtney's curiosity was roused.

"Waylon couldn't have been killed very long before Johnny arrived." A smug look graced her face.

"Why do you say that?"

"Most of the guys left work between seven and eight this evening. Right?"

"Right. Four hours before Johnny came to see him." Courtney didn't see how four hours was close to the time Johnny arrived.

"But what did Johnny say when the sheriff asked him questions?"

Courtney cast her mind back over the conversation. It had hardly been an interrogation. Well, maybe a soft interrogation. "He asked where Johnny had been, and Tyson gave him an alibi."

"Almost. He could have gotten to Waylon's house, killed him, and ran here. He had time to do that much." Patty's tone had grown serious. "He's not totally out of the woods as far as timing. Unless the coroner or medical examiner, or whoever does those kind of things, says Waylon was killed at least an hour before Johnny got there."

"But you said… I'm confused." Courtney's mind wasn't going wherever Patty tried to lead her.

"Johnny said he received a text from Waylon, he had one more drink, and then he and Tyson left the bar. Whatever Waylon learned, he found out right before he texted Johnny. So, he was still alive about a half hour before Johnny arrived. The time it takes to have one more drink, pay the bill, get in Tyson's truck, arrive at Waylon's house."

By Courtney's calculations, the bar was only a few blocks away. It couldn't take more than five minutes to get from the bar to anywhere else in Elm City. Everything was so close. So, from the bar to Waylon's would only take five minutes.

"How would someone know Waylon texted Johnny?" Courtney asked. "Isn't that what you're saying? They planned it so Johnny would take the blame?"

"Maybe. Or maybe whatever Waylon had discovered couldn't get out, and they wanted to keep him quiet. Or someone used Waylon's phone to get Johnny on the scene in time to be the prime suspect." The grim set to Patty's mouth indicated her anger at the guilty party.

"Horrible. Either way, Johnny's in trouble. I don't think they'll be able to tell exactly when Waylon was killed, and a half hour won't make a difference in their estimate."

"Exactly. We can't let him take the blame." Patty stood up. "I need to get going. I'm usually up at four o'clock getting the diner ready. Not sure these old bones can get up after only a few hours of sleep."

"You're not old." They walked to the door.

She sighed. "I've aged tonight." She opened the door to leave.

"Let me know if I can help with anything," Courtney told her. "And if you find out anything new. I'm going to be doing some searching myself."

"Be careful," Patty said.

"You too." Courtney watched her walk to her car, and after she drove off, she stepped inside and locked the door behind her. For the first time since she'd arrived in Elm City, she was nervous about being alone. Life didn't feel safe.

CHAPTER 18

Courtney woke up when Alex crawled into bed. "Tough, huh?"

"Yeah." He pulled her close and held her.

She realized his hair was wet. "Is it raining?"

"No. I took a shower when I got home."

She felt guilty she'd slept through his immediate return, but maybe he appreciated a few minutes with no conversation or other distractions.

"We need to be there for Lori," Alex said. "Johnny was right. She was hysterical. They called a doctor to see what to do for her. Their parents were silent at first, until they learned Waylon was murdered. Then his mother started crying, and his father stared at the floor, trying to hide his feelings until we left."

"How did they treat Johnny?"

"Well enough. They hugged him tightly, and their mother even told him she loved him. Which only a loving mother would do."

"And the police didn't arrest him?" She was still concerned Johnny was their number one suspect, although she had no idea why he would kill his twin. They seemed to get along fine at the construction site.

"No." He moved away slightly so he could see her face.

The room was dark except for the slight glow from the nightlight in the hallway. Courtney was ashamed she was slightly afraid of the dark and started using the nightlight when Alex was in prison. She couldn't make out the expression in his eyes, but she could tell from the shape of his mouth he was frowning.

"I don't believe Johnny killed him. Do you?" he asked.

"No. But you know how they always suspect the person who finds the body? That was Johnny. I considered calling Nathan."

She could see the shake of his head and guessed what he was going to say. "That's not necessary. They'll need more evidence than

Johnny finding the body to arrest him. A motive. A weapon. It's going to take a while."

She breathed a sigh of relief. "I guess I need to rein in my imagination."

"I love your imagination. They had him change clothes at his house and took the ones he was wearing. I drove his vehicle to the farm and stood in the background while they told his parents and Lori." Alex stretched out and rearranged his pillow. "Why don't we get some sleep? It's already 4:30 a.m. We should get to the construction site by eight instead of six to make a statement to the construction workers."

"Right. All the activity on the street indicated something happened, so we might as well show up a little later than usual. I'm sure somebody saw the body bag. I'd rather listen to what they have to say first thing, but to be honest, my body has reached its limit for the week. Too much hard labor. My brain is tired too. And a murder on top of it all." She snuggled next to him. "Good night. I love you."

"I love you too."

They kissed and settled into a close embrace. Courtney knew Alex dreaded the next day as much as she did.

***

Courtney wandered around the construction site the next morning after Alex gave his early morning speech, praising Waylon's work and his commitment to family. They had a moment of prayerful silence for him, and then everyone got to work.

There wasn't much talk for the first half of the day. Gradually, occasional conversations broke out after lunch. Johnny hadn't appeared for work, and Courtney hadn't expected him to come to the site. She assumed he was home with his parents and sister.

Her first indication something was wrong was Gary's appearance. She stood outside enjoying the cool, fresh air, trying to do anything to stay awake. Holding a Dr. Pepper in one hand and her cell phone in the other, she watched Gary pull up in his own vehicle.

When he got out of his pickup, she noticed he wasn't in uniform.

"How's it going today?" he asked.

"Fine. Little slow to start, but everyone's working now. Johnny hasn't shown up, which doesn't surprise me."

"Me neither. However, the sheriff can't find him."

Courtney couldn't hide her surprise. Johnny seemed committed to his family. She remembered his concern over Lori. "Are you saying he left his family the day after his brother's death, and they don't know where he is?"

"That's what they said."

Something in his tone made her study his face. "You think they know where he is. Is he hiding so he doesn't get arrested?"

"The idea crossed our minds."

She shook her head. "I can't believe it."

"So you say, Courtney. But you always believe the best of people." Gary nodded in understanding. "Not a put-down. It's refreshing."

She almost stamped her foot on the ground. "I'm not naïve, Gary. I'm actually concerned something happened to him. Maybe he went on a bender and hurt himself.”

“You don’t need to worry,” he said wryly. “His family isn’t bothered, and they would be after what happened to Waylon.”

She agreed. “Okay. You’re right. What’s he doing, and why won’t they tell anyone? Does he have any friends who would know where he could hide out? He drinks with Tyson, but I don’t believe they’re close friends.”

“I don’t think they’re close enough for Johnny to hide out there. They’re drinking buddies with only one thing in common,” Gary said.

Courtney nodded. “The local bar. Is Tyson serious about sticking around here and farming?”

“Definitely. He loves the farm,” Gary said.

She stared at the shiny red vehicle Tyson drove. “What if Waylon found out something about the jewels? Would Tyson hang around Johnny, hoping to hear some information? He loves to flaunt his money.”

Gary smiled wryly. “Most guys do at that age. Or at any age. I remember when I got to fly the best planes in the Air Force. Gave me a big head, until the next guy got his turn."

"Do you fly now?" Courtney asked.

"Sometimes. When I get a little time, there's a plane nearby a friend owns. He lets me borrow it when I want to get some time in the air. It's certainly different than flying under duress. I could go for a plane equal to Tyson's truck." He smiled at her. "If you ever want to fly, tell me. I'd take Alex up too, of course."

"I'll keep it in mind when we get caught up with this project. What do you think about Tyson's time with Johnny?" Courtney asked.

"I'm not sure. Someone to go out with to unwind?" Gary suggested.

"Maybe. There's quite an age difference. Fifteen years." Tyson was only seventeen when the Millers were murdered, but he wasn't out of the running for Waylon's death.

"Drinking buddies don't care about age," Gary said.

Courtney didn't answer as she watched a car speeding down the road. It turned at their driveway. She hadn't seen many cars drive past the inn, but she'd seen this vehicle last night. It was Patty's brown sedan. "Why's she here?"

Gary frowned as Patty jumped from her car and slammed the door.

"I have to talk to you," she panted, out of breath from running to where they stood in front of the house. She noticed one of the workers, Robb, getting a soda from the cooler and waited for him to go back inside.

CHAPTER 19

Courtney stared in fascination at Patty's flushed face. "Do you want to talk to me alone, or can Gary stay?"

"Oh, Gary can certainly stay. I need his help too. The whole community should help." Patty's hurried speech caused her to slur her words.

"Hey, slow down." Courtney led her to one of the chairs set up by the coolers full of beverages. "Sit down here. Do you need something to drink?" She lifted the lid and took out a bottle of water.

Gary took a cola, and Patty sat down on one of the chairs but tapped her foot impatiently. "I don't want anything to drink. I need to know where Johnny is."

"Why do you need to find him?" Courtney had never seen her so riled up.

"Because he's in danger. I'm in danger." She glanced around, but the others were working inside. They had fifteen minutes before the break brought them outside.

"What do you mean?" Gary stopped drinking and stared at her.

"Why?" Courtney echoed.

Patty suddenly closed her mouth after having been eager to get their attention. "I need to find him."

"No one will tell us." Courtney took a long drink of water.

"Someone must know where he is," she said desperately.

"Well…someone does," Gary told her. "But they haven't told us. Have you gone to his parents or Lori and asked them?"

"They didn't tell me anything, but I believe he's been in contact with them. They were too relaxed to be worried if he was missing."

"Why wouldn't they tell you?" Courtney was surprised. She figured everyone in the town would share information with Patty. Especially the Fredericksons.

"They think I'll tell someone else, but I wouldn't. Not in this case." Her face flushed. "I gossip a bit, but there's a lot more I know that's really secret, and I never share. Never have. Never will."

"Never's a long time." Gary's lips twisted.

Was he thinking about his parents and his eight-year-long search? "You're going to have to tell us what's going on. We can certainly keep your secret. And if your life and his are in danger, someone needs to be aware of it." Courtney didn't add, *in case something happens to you, and we need a suspect to interrogate.*

Their silence lasted a few minutes while the birds sang, and the wind blew the few leaves that had migrated to the front of the house from the one tree in the backyard. It should have been peaceful. Instead, the fatigue of the late night and the strain of Patty's silence drained her.

Patty finally sighed. "Okay. But only among the three of us. Agreed?"

Courtney nodded right away, but Gary studied her closely. "Will I need to report this to the sheriff?"

She nodded in frustration. "At some point."

At that moment, the inn doors flew open, and Doug and Tyson tumbled out the door.

"Don't come back in until you get it figured out," Honor yelled at them. She nodded to Courtney, Gary, and Patty before going back inside.

Their presence seemed to have a cooling effect on Tyson and Doug.

"What's this about, guys?" Gary asked them.

Tyson pointed his finger at Doug. "He's saying I killed Waylon. I couldn't have done it. I was with Johnny all night. I picked Johnny up at Waylon's house. Waylon was alive when we left. We were together until I dropped Johnny off at Waylon's at midnight. He went into the house, and the minute the lights went on, I left. So, get off my back, Doug."

"You left him at Waylon's house?" Courtney asked, already aware of the answer. It occurred to her she should check Tyson's story. "Why didn't you drop him off at his own house?"

"He said something about him and Waylon finishing some discussion. And he got a text while we were drinking."

Patty took in a quick breath.

Courtney believed it had to do with the secret Patty was holding back. Patty was already aware of the text, so why was it a sudden shock to her? Maybe it was the part about finishing a discussion. Like they'd started talking about something, and Waylon had new information.

Doug laughed. "Right. You both went back to Waylon's and murdered him."

When Tyson's hand bunched into a fist, Gary leapt up and stood between them. "Both of you, back up six paces."

The anger on Tyson's face didn't dissipate, but he did step back.

Doug continued to smirk.

When Gary turned to him, Doug lost the smirk and backed up. "Why are you so sure they did it together?"

"Because they wanted something Waylon had." Doug balled his fists together.

"What did he have?" Gary's hand dropped to his side now the two men appeared to be acting more civilized.

Doug threw a glance of triumph at Gary. "Your parents' jewels."

Patty gasped and sat up straight. Her mouth hung open.

"How do you know that?" Gary's measured tone sounded reflective.

"It makes sense," Doug said. "Why else would someone murder Waylon?"

"Why, indeed?" Gary asked. "But at the moment, you have no proof he had the jewels. Right?"

Doug's shoulders slumped. "Right."

"So, all this is conjecture, and you're running your mouth off about people's reputations, with no idea what you're saying."

"Pretty much," Tyson answered for him.

Doug straightened. The tension returned.

"Enough," Gary said. "Guessing and blaming isn't going to help the situation. If you have real proof, let's hear it. Otherwise, get back to work. I'm sure Alex and Courtney aren't paying you to fight."

"Definitely not," Courtney confirmed. "You've taken over the plumbing, Doug, which was our original arrangement before we hired Waylon. Just want you to be aware, I have no problem firing anyone, even the forewoman's husband if I have to. Let's not go down that road."

Without looking back, Doug slunk into the building. Tyson waited a few minutes and then followed.

"Well," Gary said.

"Indeed." Courtney turned to Patty. "This is where you come in."

CHAPTER 20

Patty's face glowed red, and Courtney reached into the cooler then passed her a bottle of water. As she twisted the lid off with shaky hands, Gary watched with interest.

"So, the jewelry. My mom had a lot of expensive items. One day, she showed me everything. There was a diamond necklace, a ruby necklace, a sapphire necklace, and an emerald necklace. She said she had one for every occasion." His voice softened at the memories.

"She had matching earrings and bracelets for each. Plus, there was an assortment of rings. The rings were her favorite. She seemed fine with the rest of her jewelry, but she was always adding a new ring here or there. Some were costume jewelry; some were expensive. It was more the meaning behind the rings that kept her attached to them. She'd buy them for special occasions, or my father would buy them for her as presents. It was a running joke between them as to who bought the most rings during their time together.

"My last memory of a ring-buying adventure happened before I joined the Air Force. I didn't have much money. My parents believed in me earning a living but still gave me what I needed. I had a summer job and saved up to give my mom a pearl ring. I gave it to her the night before I left for Air Force training. Yes, it was small and inexpensive, but she stared at it for the longest time and started crying. I knew what she was thinking but would never say. Her son was joining the military, and things happen. I might never return, and that would be her last memento.

"She dried her tears and told me it was beautiful. Her favorite ring ever." He grinned, although Courtney caught a sheen of tears in his eyes. Her own weren't dry either. "She always said that when she got a new ring: 'my favorite ever.'"

"I'm guessing she meant it," Courtney said.

"I think so too." He nodded and stared at Patty. "So, the jewels. Where are they?"

"My house." Her hands twisted together. "Waylon dug them up the first night the structural crew finished for the day. He went out there when he was sure everyone was gone. Then he brought them to me the next day and told me to keep them for him. I have a safe at home, which most people don't know. They assume since I have one at the diner, I don't need another one. He planned to give them back to you, but he told me he figured out who killed your parents. He said he had a question only the murderer had the answer to, and he was going to ask them first."

"Why?" Courtney exploded. "Why not turn the jewelry over to the sheriff and Gary right away? Didn't he realize how dangerous his plan was? The murderer already killed two people."

"I asked him that. All he said was he had to be sure he was right. He didn't want to accuse the wrong person." Patty's eyes filled with tears as she looked at Gary. "I almost called you the minute he left the jewels with me and walked out to his vehicle."

She stared down at her hands, finally still. "I should have. I'll never forgive myself."

Courtney patted her on the shoulder and gave her a hug. "You can't blame yourself." She stared at Gary.

"I guess I have to find out where Waylon went after he talked to you."

"A whole week passed between when he talked to me and when he was killed." Courtney shook her head. "He probably saw everyone in town during that time."

"He's not very social," Patty said. "Everyone thinks Johnny keeps to himself, except when he's drinking, but Waylon is—I mean was— worse. He'd work and go home."

"Then it shouldn't be too hard to find out his movements." He stood there. "First thing we're going to do is pick up the jewelry from your house. I'll have the sheriff meet us there."

Patty stood up and wobbled. Courtney caught her.

"Thanks. I've been so tense. My legs were shaking." She turned to Gary. "I didn't want to say anything in front of Johnny. I don't know how much Waylon told him. Am I in trouble?"

"We can rule you out," Gary said. "It's a good thing you came to tell us. That will go a long way toward the sheriff's leniency."

"I did peek in the container. They're lovely." She sighed. "I didn't touch anything, except the outside of the box and the clasp. Waylon told me not to."

"Did he say how he came to have them?" Gary asked.

"He said your mother told him where to find the jewels if something happened to her and your father."

They made their way back to each of their vehicles. They had parked far enough away to allow room for the workers to maneuver and get their tools into and out of the building easier.

Courtney stopped suddenly. "Valerie Miller told Waylon where she hid her jewelry?"

"That's what he said. Something about how scared she was someone would steal them. She hadn't told anyone about them when she first moved to Elm City. She started wearing her expensive bracelets, and she wore a necklace and bracelet set to an event in Dickinson. Honor took a picture, and everyone saw it," Patty said.

"It was all over town within a day," Patty continued. "I'm not sure why they thought there were more than what she wore to that event. Waylon was careful not to tell Johnny. He was always afraid Johnny would give away the secret when he was drunk."

"Which might have happened," Courtney said. "Johnny could have come across the jewelry in Waylon's hiding place and told someone else."

"Maybe that's why they were fighting the other day." Patty covered her mouth in horror. "I didn't mean…Johnny would never kill Waylon, no matter what their fight was about. It was after Waylon dug up the jewels, but he said I was the only one he'd told. He only had them one day before he gave them to me to put in my safe. It's not likely Johnny found them in one night."

Courtney realized Gary was soaking up every ounce of their speculations. What could be proven was another matter. She hoped Patty's revelation wouldn't cause her problems with the police. She believed her story. "Did Waylon tell you where he found the jewels when Gary's parents went missing?"

"Valerie hid them behind the rickety shed in the backyard. They were halfway between the corner of the shed and one lonely tree. Waylon went out there the first evening when the Dickinson crew left for the day. He wanted to see if the jewels were still there. When they were, he took them and hid them overnight, then brought them to me right after work."

Courtney remembered the hole back there when they'd seen the other holes in the backyard. "Did he mention other holes dug in the backyard?"

"He dug up the jewels a few nights before you found those other holes. He figured no one local would be around if he waited for Honor to leave after checking out the site. He went sometime in the middle of the night, just to be sure."

"I don't see why he didn't give them to the police right away eight years ago," Gary said. "If my parents left as planned, they would definitely have taken the jewelry with them. The police might have looked closer at the people in this community instead of all over the U.S."

The anger in his voice was unmistakable. "I could have searched here sooner."

"He was afraid it would make him appear guilty." Patty appeared ready to cry again. "He might have believed the jewels were gone. The

RV and your parents were gone. He probably assumed they took them with them."

"Let's concentrate on now," Courtney said. "Waylon told Patty last week. She thought he would tell the police when he confirmed the identity of the murderer. She never anticipated he'd be murdered too. Waylon's information is beyond our reach, but his killer, and probably your parents' killer, are still out there. Let's focus."

Gary shook his head. "I'll call the sheriff on the way to Patty's house now. He and I'll collect the jewelry, and the two of you will stay out of the investigation. As Patty said when she first arrived, she's in danger. The fact we've been out here talking all this time will get around. Now you're in danger too, Courtney."

"And don't forget about Johnny," Patty reminded. "What if the reason Tyson picked him up at Waylon's before they went out last night was because Waylon told Johnny about the jewels? Johnny went out with Tyson, spilled the information about the jewels. Tyson could be guilty."

"But he was with Johnny the whole time," Courtney objected. "Unless there are two people involved, and Tyson texted his cohort, who killed Waylon and searched the place, only to come up empty."

"I haven't forgotten Johnny may have told Tyson. Or Johnny and Tyson worked together. I'm going to have to press the Fredericksons to tell us where Johnny is," Gary said.

When Gary drove away, Patty started following him in her car but stopped. Courtney's truck engine idled as Patty got out of her car and walked back to talk to her. Courtney lowered the window.

"What's up?" she asked Patty. The woman had tear stains on her face and red eyes.

"I'm going to Johnny's parents to find out where he is. Would you come with me?" she begged. "If you tell them you need to know when he'll be back, they might tell you more than me."

Could she get the Fredericksons to give up Johnny's location? She doubted it. But why not try?

"You go meet Gary at your house and do what you need to do. Maybe I'll make better headway if I go alone."

Patty looked doubtful.

"Gary and Sheriff Warren are waiting for you."

"I guess." She trudged back to her car like she was going to her execution.

It might not be an execution, but the sheriff was not going to be happy with her. Nor was he going to be happy with Courtney when he found out she was trying to find out where Johnny went.

CHAPTER 21

Courtney arrived at the Fredericksons' farm. It was average-sized and reminded her of the Langs' farmstead. The house was painted bright white, with lots of orange and yellow mums lining the steps. Some of them were filled with healthy blossoms, but a lot of them were ready to be put away for the season. Two carved pumpkins added to the mix and appeared in better shape than the flowers.

The barn and other outbuildings were all painted faded red. On purpose, she decided. She kind of liked the way it appeared homier than the bright red barns she'd seen.

She knocked on the front door, not knowing who would answer. Lori had graduated in the spring. Did she have a job? Or did she work on the farm? What did Patty tell her?

The door was opened by a man in his sixties with heavily tanned skin on his face and arms, and deep wrinkles around his eyes and forehead.

Probably from squinting against the sun for days at a time. His wrinkled short-sleeved shirt showed he'd already worked up a sweat.

"Hi." She held out her hand. "I'm Courtney Richmond. I'm remodeling the Miller house into an inn."

He shook her hand firmly. "Ed Frederickson. You hired Waylon and Johnny."

"I did. I'm so sorry about Waylon and sorry to be bothering you at a time like this."

He glanced back into the house for a minute as if looking for an escape or someone else to come rescue him. "Elaine is lying down right now. Has a bit of a headache. I have no idea where Lori is. Probably riding her horse. It helps her calm down when she's upset."

"That's okay," Courtney told him, sorry she'd come when the family was grieving. How had Patty talked her into this?

"But you didn't come to find out what everyone's doing." He eyed her shrewdly. "How can I help you?"

"Can you tell me where I can find Johnny? I'd like to have him come back to work and do the electrical wiring, but I can't find him. He probably doesn't want to work immediately, which is fine. If I can get an estimated timeframe when or if he wants to work, it would be helpful. It's hard to get good electrical help out here."

He gave a sad smile at her last comment. "Johnny is great at that. In fact, I'm not one to brag, but he's brilliant. He instinctively knows what to do."

"That's what I found in the few days I've worked with him so far," Courtney nodded, "which is why I want him back. When he's ready, of course."

Ed studied her for a minute. "You look like you can keep a secret."

Oh no. What was he going to tell her?

"I'll tell you under one condition. You tell no one. And I mean no one. Not Patty. Not the police. Not Gary. He wants to find out what happened to his parents. I want to find out what happened to Waylon, but both of us are going to have to wait a little longer. Johnny's in no condition to talk at the moment. When he's ready, we'll get more out of him."

"I have my own stipulation. I want to tell my husband. He can keep a secret as well as I can, but we don't keep secrets from each other," Courtney said. "If that's a deal breaker, I guess I'll have to wait with the rest of Elm City for Johnny's return."

A small smile lit Ed's eyes before sadness dropped over his gaze. "Fair enough. It's a deal. Johnny came to stay with us last night, and we had a long talk. He blames himself for Waylon's death although he had nothing to do with it. But that's the way it is with those two. Always protecting each other. Waylon tried to stop him from drinking, but he never could. A man has to decide for himself when he's done enough damage.

"He reached that point last night. After we talked, he told us he was going to the alcoholics' rehabilitation center in Dickinson to quit drinking. He said he'd tell the clinic he had a week, and then needed to get back to Elm City. He's hospitalized while they keep an eye on him and physically stop the drinking. Then…" he trailed off, "he plans to come back and find out what happened to Waylon."

Courtney sympathized with the man's concern. A week wasn't very long to overcome a drinking problem that had lasted years.

"He can do it," Ed said. "His brother's death triggered something in him. Well, I hope it lasts. We can only pray it works."

"I'll pray too," Courtney assured him. "And he has a job with us whenever he's ready. Neither Alex nor I believe he did anything wrong. That will come out when the truth is known. We're close to learning what happened to the Millers and Waylon."

"Thank you."

She'd found out what was going on. Johnny planned to get sober and find Waylon's killer. She hoped it wasn't for revenge.

Ed started to close the door when a teenage girl appeared behind him. She had beautiful straight blond hair and red-rimmed deep blue eyes. She was pretty and as tall as Courtney.

"Wait a minute, Dad. Who is she?" she asked.

"Waylon and Johnny's boss," he told her. "She needs to get going."

The teenager barged past him and stared at Courtney. "Hi. I'm Lori."

"Hi, Lori. It's nice to meet you." She sympathized with the young girl who had shadows in her eyes. "I'm sorry about your brother. He was a fine man," she said gently.

"Can we talk for a few minutes?" Lori asked shyly. "Dad said you were leaving…"

"That's okay. I'm not in any hurry."

Lori slipped outside. Her feet were bare, but she didn't care. "Let's go see the goats. They're always fun to show visitors." She glanced back at her dad. "I'll be back in a bit."

He appeared doubtful but didn't say anything as Courtney turned to follow Lori, who was already several feet ahead of her.

"Don't you want shoes?" Courtney watched for animal deposits around the area. She'd been careful where she stepped, but the well-landscaped yard had so far been free of anything yucky.

"No. We're not going in the pen. They'll be playing outside today, and we can see through the fence."

They reached a wooden pen high enough to keep the goats inside. When Courtney peeked over the fence, she witnessed six cute little goats frolicking around the enclosure. There were a few with combination black-and-white fur. One of them was totally light brown except for a white circle of fur around one eye. And the rest were black with random white patches of fur.

"They're fainting goats." Lori looked at Courtney. "Have you ever heard of them?"

"No. Why are they called that?"

"If they are scared, they'll drop into what we call a faint. It doesn't hurt them, and within a few minutes, they're back on their feet." She let out a sudden yell, making Courtney jump.

One of the goats fell over and lay there. He appeared dead. "Is he okay?"

Lori laughed. "Yes. And he's actually a she. I don't usually scare them. It's kind of cruel, so I only do it to show people what happens. See, she's getting up."

Indeed, the goat got to her feet and was soon playing with the others.

"Wow. That is so cool." Was "cool" still a word to use?

"Yes. It's interesting." She leaned her back against the fence, studying Courtney. "Do you know what happened to my brother? You told my dad the answers were close."

How could she tell Lori it was based on a feeling, not actual evidence? "There are a lot of us searching for answers. The sheriff's department. Gary is especially invested because of his parents."

"And you're looking." Lori stared at her.

"And I'm looking. But maybe you shouldn't be telling anyone about my interest." Courtney returned her stare.

"It's too late to be a secret. You've gone around asking questions, and people pay attention to anything to do with the disappearance."

Courtney burst into laughter. "You're so smart. Of course it's not going to stay a secret if a teenage girl knows. Small towns. It's like being in a kiddie pool. One person whispers, and everyone hears."

Lori smiled, but her eyes remained sad. "Exactly."

"You must have lots of friends to talk to, but if you ever need someone, you can call me. Your parents also seem like they want to take care of you, so don't block them out. Let them help you, if they want. It'll do them good."

"You're right." She sighed. "I don't want them to smother me, so I hope you find out who killed Waylon soon."

"I understand. You want to be on your own. What are your plans when school ends?"

"I want to be an electrician. Johnny's going to help me."

"Hey, terrific." Courtney couldn't imagine any of her classmates wanting to follow that path when they were younger. "You must be pretty close to him."

"I am. He and I lived with Waylon keeping us in line. We always joked about it." She shook her head. "It's not funny anymore. I wish he was back telling us what to do." Tears filled her eyes.

"I'm sorry." Courtney wished she could do something more for Lori.

"I'll be okay." She wiped her eyes with the back of her hand. "Johnny will be back in a week, and hopefully sober. Waylon would be pleased to see how Johnny has pulled himself together. At least I believe Waylon can see what's happening from Heaven."

"Oh, I believe that too. And you're right. Waylon will be proud of him. Like Waylon's proud of his sister."

She nodded and headed back toward the house. "Thank you for listening. Please tell me if you find out anything?" She framed it as a question.

"I will, but the police will probably get the information before I do. They'll tell your parents. But if you have questions, you can call me."

"Thanks."

They had reached Courtney's truck, and she got in and waved to Lori. The teenager watched her from the top step into the house.

Now Courtney had to somehow satisfy Patty's curiosity without telling her the whole truth since she'd promised not to tell anyone except Alex where Johnny was.

CHAPTER 22

Courtney stopped at Patty's house after she finished talking to Ed Frederickson. How was she going to tell Patty she'd promised to keep the details about Johnny secret?

A police SUV parked in front of Patty's house stood out. Courtney had seen a few curtains twitching as she drove her own pickup down the street a little farther to park. As she walked up the sidewalk to Patty's house, she recognized Patty's car parked in the driveway. The lawn and flowers were brown and shriveled under a carpet of leaves. Only a few leaves hugged the branches on the elm tree gracing the front yard.

When she knocked on the front door, it took a few minutes for Patty to appear. The screen door opened, and she invited her in. "They're studying the jewels now," she whispered as Courtney followed her down the short hallway.

They turned into a small room holding a red-and-blue plaid sofa and matching stuffed armchairs. Between the chairs and couch, a coffee table glittered with a pile of jewelry in a decorated dark brown box. The sheriff and Gary wore gloves as they peered inside.

"They're not touching them until they can check for fingerprints," Patty explained.

"Oh." She was mesmerized by the top necklace. Brilliant emeralds bracketed in silver shone even in the dim light of Patty's living room. The closed curtains meant only the ceiling light illuminated the room. "They're beautiful."

Gary stared up at her. "They're definitely my mom's jewelry. Why did Waylon wait to dig them up?"

They all turned to Patty. "When Waylon heard Courtney and Alex asking questions, he got nervous. He said it was time to check if the jewels were still where Mrs. Miller had told him."

She repeated some of what she told them before, but they listened.

"When did you say Waylon gave them to you?" Sheriff Warren asked.

"A few days before the bones were found." She shivered. "I'm glad you're taking them. I don't want them here, as beautiful as they are."

"We'll make it obvious we've found the jewels and have them secured," the sheriff told her. "Let's see what happens. We'll find a few people ready to talk about a few other people."

"Turn them against each other?" Courtney asked. "It's a safer alternative than having everyone believe the jewels can still be found for anyone to take."

The sheriff closed the lid of the jewelry box and put the whole thing into a paper bag. He folded the top and taped it, pulled out a pen and initialed the tape. He handed the pen to Gary, who also initialed the tape before handing the pen back to the sheriff.

The sheriff pushed the bag aside, so he had a better view of Patty sitting across from him on the sofa. "I have a question for you, Patty. You mentioned Tyson picked Johnny up at Waylon's house last night."

"That's what Johnny said sometime last night when he was here. I'm guessing Waylon told Johnny about the jewels before Tyson picked him up." She glanced at Courtney for confirmation.

"Someone said Tyson picked Johnny up at Waylon's house, but I don't remember who said it. I think it was Johnny." Courtney's eyes blurred from fatigue, and she wanted to go home and take a nap despite the excitement of getting closer to answers.

"So, Johnny and Tyson could have killed Waylon and then gone out. When they returned, Johnny raised the alarm," Gary said.

They watched Patty's reaction.

She was shaking her head the whole time he talked. "No. Johnny did not kill Waylon."

"You can't be sure," Courtney said gently. "When people drink, they do things they wouldn't ordinarily do."

Patty stood up indignantly and stared down at them. "No way! That man, no matter what, would not kill his twin brother. If Waylon had a bruise on his body, I'd buy Johnny hitting him, but that's not the case."

"He looked pretty relaxed sitting on the couch with the stab wound." The sheriff stared back at her.

The sheriff's words describing the scene to Patty, who was already overwrought, were harsh.

Of course, he was searching for the truth, not hosting a tea party.

"What?" Patty asked, surprise lifting her brows. "Someone stabbed him? Wasn't he shot?"

"What made you think that?" the sheriff asked sharply.

"I don't know." Patty's brow wrinkled. "I assumed that's what happened. Someone planned to kill Waylon, so they brought along a gun."

"Maybe it wasn't planned." Courtney touched her lightly on the arm. "Maybe it was a spur-of-the-moment thing."

"Not Johnny. It wasn't him." Patty's adamant statement rang in the room. "Even if it wasn't planned. He would have hit Waylon, not killed him."

"What was he stabbed with?" Courtney asked the sheriff.

A slight smile lifted his lips. "Do you think I'm sharing that information?"

She gave him a full-blown smile in response and shrugged. "I hoped."

"Keep hoping. I'm only sharing the jewel discovery to keep from finding more bodies." He stood up. "And don't pass on the stabbing information. Let others assume whatever they want."

He picked up the bag with the jewelry box, and Gary followed him out of the room. Patty trailed behind and locked up behind them.

Courtney remained sitting on the couch. The jewels were found, and Waylon was stabbed. And Johnny was quitting drinking. Did he kill his brother, and that made him finally seek help? Or seeing his brother dead made him take the step?

Patty returned and sat on one of the armchairs, plucking at the upholstery on the arm. "Johnny didn't kill Waylon." She said it softly, as if speaking to herself. Or trying to convince herself.

"Of course not," Courtney agreed. It wouldn't hurt anything for the moment. Johnny was busy for the coming week and couldn't cause any trouble if he was the actual killer. "You're a good friend. He'll need one when he returns."

Patty burst into tears. "I don't want to be his friend."

Had Courtney misunderstood? Patty had been more Waylon's friend, but she didn't appear to dislike Johnny. And why was she looking for him and standing up to the sheriff for Johnny if she didn't want to be his friend?

She knelt on the carpet beside Patty. *God, tell me what to say.* "Patty."

The woman regarded her, tears streaming from her eyes.

"I don't understand why you don't want to be his friend. Don't you like him? I mean, you loved Waylon. Is that why you put up with Johnny?"

"You've got it all wrong." Her voice came out clogged with tears. "I need a tissue."

Courtney searched the room.

"In the kitchen," Patty told her.

She'd never been to Patty's house before, but she left the room and went in the direction she assumed the kitchen would be, across the hall and a little closer to the front door. She didn't see any tissues, but she found a roll of paper towels. She took the whole roll and handed it to Patty.

After wiping and blowing her nose, Patty sat back and sighed. "This has been a long day."

"Very long." Courtney resumed her seat on the couch as Patty got herself back together.

Patty looked at her. "You're the first person I'm telling this to."

CHAPTER 23

Courtney couldn't imagine what new information she was going to be absorbing next. Patty wasn't kidding when she said she was full of secrets.

"I went to school here in Elm City with the Frederickson twins. I told you. What I didn't tell you was Waylon and I dated for a short time. It didn't take us very long to realize we were meant to be only friends.

"Johnny started drinking around that time, and we both tried to steer him away from that life. There's only so much you can do for another person, although Waylon never gave up hope."

Courtney nodded. "Yes, there is."

"For a year or so, the two brothers tried to have separate groups of friends. Something hard to do in a small town. There aren't enough people. As time went on, their groups overlapped, and soon they were back to being the twins who were always together. That hasn't changed since then. Why Waylon felt responsible for Johnny's drinking, I don't know, but with Waylon gone, Johnny will be lost."

Courtney couldn't decide if it was fatigue, but she was still lost about Patty's declaration she didn't want to be Johnny's friend. *Ask*, she told herself. "So, why don't you want to be Johnny's friend?"

"I want it to be more." Patty ducked her head, and Courtney watched a blush spread across the back of her neck. "I'm in love with Johnny. I've loved him ever since I realized Waylon and I could only be friends, and he wasn't the twin I wanted. But Johnny never showed any interest in me. So, here I am. Almost forty, single, and pining for a man who doesn't have a clue I'm there for him."

"I'm sorry, Patty."

Whoa. That was why Patty wanted to find Johnny. And it explained her defense of him and her belief he couldn't be Waylon's killer.

"Have you ever approached Johnny to see if he feels the same way? He might think he can't make a move because you dated Waylon."

Patty gazed into the distance. "It crossed my mind a lot. But there's another aspect to consider.

My mother was an alcoholic. I don't know if I want to live with another one."

Courtney understood. "Living like that…it's unstable."

"You do understand." She heaved another sigh. "It's been a long time since I've even considered approaching Johnny. And now he's disappeared." She sat up and stared at Courtney hopefully. "Did you find out anything when you went out to see the Fredericksons?"

"Ed answered the door. He said Elaine was lying down." She stopped. How could she phrase the next part without lying?

"What about Johnny?" Patty asked impatiently.

"Ed said he's fine and in a safe place."

Patty frowned. "That's not a lot of information."

"He's safe, Patty. He'll be back, and you can talk everything out with him." She'd at least managed not to lie.

"How can I tell him now that Waylon's dead?" she wailed.

"What does that have to do with it? Johnny could use your friendship now more than ever.

And maybe he's wanted more all these years too. Wouldn't you rather find out how he feels about you, so you can move on with your life?" Courtney would have been driven to a frenzy waiting twenty years for a resolution with Alex.

"He'll believe I'm trying to help him because Waylon's gone. He won't understand I've loved him all these years." Patty's face was limp from exhaustion.

"Okay. Enough. We're going to stop thinking about all this right now. You need some sleep, and so do I. We both have to be at work tomorrow. I can't run around all day expecting everyone else to do all the work." Actually, she could, but Patty needed to rest. She stood up.

Patty stood up too and walked her to the door.

"Who ran the diner for you today?" she asked.

"My friend Lucy. She fills in for me when I'm sick or something comes up where I need help."

"That's good." Courtney opened the front door. "You're going to be okay but call me if you need to talk."

"I will."

"Promise me you'll change into comfy clothes, find some television program or book or something to occupy you. Eat some food and go to bed. There's nothing more you can do tonight."

"Okay." Patty hung on to the doorknob, like she'd fall if she let go.

"Promise?" Courtney persisted.

"Promise."

"Okay. I'll talk to you tomorrow, unless you need to call tonight."

"Thank you, Courtney." Patty closed the door.

The lock clicked into place, and she walked down to her car. She'd heard some dings on her phone while she'd been with Patty. As soon as she sat in the driver's seat, she pulled her phone from her pocket.

Alex called a few times asking where she was. His last text was a plea to call him and let him know she was okay. He must have forgotten about the tracking device on their phones.

He answered on the first ring. "Where are you?" he asked frantically. "I've been so worried about you."

"I'm sorry." It took a lot for him to be this concerned. She wasn't used to keeping him informed, and they were getting back into the habit since he'd been gone for two years. "I didn't mean to worry you."

His deep, relieved breath came through the phone. "You can take care of yourself, but with a murderer running around, I let my imagination take over."

"It's okay. I totally understand." And she did. If she couldn't reach Alex for a few hours, and she didn't know where he was, she'd be concerned too.

"You left the site with the police and Patty. Something happen there?" he asked.

"You're not going to believe this. Valerie Miller told Waylon where the jewels were hidden. He dug them up and gave them to Patty to hold."

"Wow. Hey, the hole behind the shed, right?"

"Exactly," Courtney said. "Mrs. Miller told him where they were hidden. I'm not sure why, out of everyone in the area, she trusted him, but she did."

"Wild." Alex's voice shifted. "I need to move to a different location. Give me a minute."

A swoosh, then a slam.

"Had to get into my truck. Some of the guys came out of the building, and I didn't want them to hear. Where are the jewels now?"

"The sheriff picked them up and took them. Patty's relieved to have them out of her house. I'm leaving her place now."

"I'd be a nervous wreck if I had them with a killer running loose."

"Exactly. I would have given them to the sheriff last night, if I were her," Courtney told him. Thinking about the jewels while she tried to sleep would have been impossible. She wouldn't have even gotten the few hours she managed to get. Maybe Patty hadn't either.

"Incredible. I guess we know why someone killed Waylon," Alex said.

"Yes, but not who."

"Maybe Johnny? Wouldn't you tell your twin brother if you had the jewelry stashed somewhere?" he asked.

"Not if he were a drinker with loose lips," she answered. "The sheriff and Gary did bring that up to Patty, but she wasn't having any such nonsense. She told them if fists were flying, she could see the brothers fighting, but she couldn't see Johnny stabbing his brother."

"Waylon was stabbed?" Alex's voice came through louder than before.

"Yes. Which is a secret the sheriff doesn't want to get out, so I didn't tell you."

He laughed, a shaky chuckle. "Right. Anything else?"

"I doubt if Waylon had anything to do with the Millers' murder. He knew where to dig up the jewels. If he had buried the Millers, he wouldn't have left the jewels there for eight years and dug holes all over the yard, which would point to him."

"True," he said.

"Are you almost done there, or are you hanging out until everyone leaves?" she asked.

"I'm leaving early. Honor has it all under control, and I need some rest," he told her.

"Good. I'll cook some steaks and potatoes on the grill, so be home in an hour." She smiled to herself, relieved the day was nearly finished, and they could crash on the couch and then the bed.

"My mouth is watering already. I'll be there with my news." He hung up.

She looked down at her phone and smiled. How like him. But she hadn't told him everything yet either. The news about Johnny and Patty could wait.

CHAPTER 24

Courtney and Alex enjoyed the perfect evening on their small deck. After the grilled steak and potatoes, they each sipped at their hot chocolate. They hadn't discussed anything about the murders.

"It's so peaceful," she murmured in the twilight.

"And now we're going to ruin the ambiance with talk of murder and jewels," Alex muttered.

She sent him a reproachful glance.

He grinned. "Too soon?"

She smiled. "Okay. You brought it up. What happened at the construction site I need to know about?"

"The sheriff came by with a search warrant to collect every screwdriver on the site."

She choked on her drink as she swallowed. After her coughing fit ended, she asked, "Do they think that's the murder weapon?"

"I assume so." His smug expression morphed into concern. "We need to figure out who killed Waylon and the Millers. We can't keep this crew together with a murderer on site. Plus, I can't afford to have them all complaining about running to the nearest hardware store to replace their tools. Some of the tools have family sentimental value. And some are superstitious about their favorite screwdriver. Most of them had a fit."

"Anyone who didn't appear to care?" Courtney asked him.

"Honor, Doug, and Robb all seemed to take it in stride. Honor was a little miffed about the pause in work, but she didn't care about her own tools. Doug basically laughed, and Robb shrugged."

"I like Robb." And his cute miniature ponies. He didn't fit the image of a killer when she pictured those beautiful horses, but she had no experience.

"Me too. He goes with the flow and never makes waves. The atmosphere around him is usually peaceful, and when it's not, he tries to bring down the tension and calm the others." Alex took a long drink of his cocoa and set the cup on the table.

"If we have any work after we're set up, we should ask if he wants to be our handyman for repairs we can't do ourselves."

"Great idea," Alex agreed.

"How long will it take to test all those screwdrivers?" Courtney looked across the yard at the fence separating them from their neighbor.

"There weren't many," Alex said. "Most of the workers had a few extras, so maybe about eighteen altogether. The police didn't collect the Phillips type."

Courtney's shoulders sagged. "Sounds exciting, but I bet they don't find anything. Who would kill someone and put the weapon back in their toolbox?"

"Good point. I hope they didn't put it in someone else's toolbox either," he said grimly.

She stared at him in horror. "That's worse."

He nodded. "Okay. What else did you learn today? You have something else burning the end of your tongue."

"You've stolen my golden moment." She frowned in mock outrage. "Patty's in love with Johnny, not Waylon."

"What?" He sat up straight. "Really?"

"Yes. Really." She relished his surprise. "She's been in love with him for years."

"What about him? Does he love her?" Alex scooted his chair to look directly at her instead of the yard.

"Neither of us know. Patty's unsure. The few times they were together, Johnny hardly glanced in her direction."

"I'd say he likes her."

She appreciated a male point of view. "Well, Patty dated Waylon for a short time in high school and before falling for Johnny. Maybe Waylon still cared for her, and Johnny didn't want to get in the middle of a reunion between the two of them."

"They're almost forty years old. If Johnny considered they liked each other all this time and didn't do anything about it, he was clueless. No sass about clueless men." Alex crossed his ankles."

"Wasn't going to say anything." She hid her smile. "Once Johnny's back, I'll have to do something about the situation."

"Maybe stay out of it?" he suggested. He held up his hands to ward off her glare. "Okay. Whatever."

"Someone needs to bring the situation to an end, one way or another."

"But why you?"

She was getting a little peeved with him. Probably because he was right, and she was tired. It wasn't her business, but she wanted to help Patty. "Because no one else will."

"I'm adding busybody to curiosity as your top traits. They're rather new, aren't they? I don't remember this side of you in Chokecherry Valley." He studied her.

"Do you mind?" She wasn't going to change to please him, but she didn't want to lose him either.

"No. I kind of like this adventurous side of you. It's because you're finally getting your dream inn. It's opened something up in you." He stepped over to her and leaned down as she looked up at him. He kissed her. "Definitely like you no matter what your new traits are."

She almost stood up and kissed him some more, but their backyard wasn't private. The hedges had lost their leaves, and the wire fence around the perimeter of the backyard only kept out the neighbor's dogs, not their view. "I like all your traits too."

He sat down again. "This may be one of our last nights to sit out here and enjoy the evening together. The weather's changing."

"I guess we'll have to enjoy time snuggling on that ugly sofa in the living room." She gazed at him with affection. "As long as we're together, our surroundings can be ugly. For a while," she added.

"For a while. They're starting on the second floor tomorrow," Alex told her. "Honor told me they can get it all closed in and the outside finished before winter hits. We can work on the inside during the winter."

"Terrific. Weren't we going to wait until spring for them to get to the second floor?"

"Some job the Dickinson guy had planned fell through, so they're rushing out here to do ours. It's a good thing we bought the materials, and they're ready to go."

She was so excited, she jumped up and kissed him again. "That's worth a few more kisses. Let's clean up the table out here and go inside. The inn's progress is going to be so amazing. I can't wait until the apartment above the inn is ready for us to live in. It's worth the lack of central air conditioning we've put up with this summer."

"Definitely," Alex agreed. "You mentioned earlier Johnny is gone. Where is he?"

"Getting sober. Something about Waylon's death led him to check into a rehabilitation center this morning. Ed and Johnny want it kept secret, so don't tell anyone."

"Wow. Good for him. My lips are sealed." He made a motion of zipping his lips.

Courtney started clearing the dishes, and Alex got up to help. "It gives me hope maybe he and Patty can get together. Part of the reason for her hesitation, besides Waylon, was Johnny's drinking problem."

CHAPTER 25
Friday, October 28th

As Courtney and Alex ate breakfast the next morning, she told him her plan. "I'm going to talk to Honor today. I want to find out who the Millers socialized with when they were here."

"What does that have to do with anything?" Alex stuck the last of his toast into his mouth and took a gulp of coffee.

"Who didn't like the Millers? Their death was probably caused by either a grudge or the jewels. The jewels seem to be the most likely reason, but I haven't looked into anything else."

"Well…" He must have caught her irritation at what she guessed he'd say next. "Be careful."

"I will. I'd take Patty with me, but she'll be busy at the diner now. It's good she's got that to occupy her until Johnny comes back."

"Are we driving separately to the inn?" he asked.

"I think so. That way, I can run errands if something's needed." She finished her own toast and eggs, slipped the dishes into the dishwasher, and grabbed her mug to fill with coffee. She hadn't quite caught up on her sleep yet, although she'd slept solidly last night. "And you can rest easy in the fact most of the suspects are probably at the construction site, so I'll be perfectly safe. I'll text you if I go visit someone at their house. And there's the tracking device on my phone."

He nodded and kissed her goodbye.

When she arrived at the inn, all the vehicles were parked close to the main road, and she had to walk a distance to reach the inn. She put on her hardhat as she watched the men up on the roof. They threw old materials down to the ground, which accounted for the parking being farther away than usual.

Honor watched the men on the roof from where she stood a few feet from Courtney's parking spot. Honor didn't look her way. "They're so quick. I wish I could run an outfit like that." Envy tinged her voice.

"You're doing a wonderful job here. Once the inn is done, you'll have that on your resume, and I bet your business will take off. You could move it to a bigger city, if you want," Courtney encouraged her, thinking if she was getting her dream, so could Honor.

Honor turned to search her expression. "True. This is going to be a beautiful place when we're finished."

"That's the plan. You keep the workers moving along, and everything will work out."

Honor smiled at her. "You're an encourager."

"Thanks." Courtney laughed. "I'll add that trait to curiosity and other things I've been called lately. And speaking of my curiosity, I have a question for you."

"Go ahead. No one needs me right now. Let's sit there." She pointed to a couple of pickups with their tailgates down.

Once they settled on the edge of a tailgate, Courtney asked, "Who were the Millers' friends? Who did they socialize with when they went out?"

Honor squinted as if staring into the distance. "Well, Doug and I occasionally went out with them. We even went to Dickinson to a symphony once. That's when Valerie wore her emerald jewels. I was awestruck. They were gorgeous."

"Who saw her wearing them?" Courtney asked her.

Honor's face closed down. "I'm not sure, but I did something I'm not proud of. I took a picture of her with my cell and showed a few other people the pictures. Sometimes, I believe that was the moment when someone decided to steal them. But I don't think they planned to kill the Millers."

"And yet, they're dead all the same." Courtney did feel bad for Honor. That must be a heavy burden to endure.

"I know. It's too late to right that wrong."

Courtney didn't want her to shut down. "Who else did they socialize with?"

"Tyson's parents, Izzy and Finn. And Brian and Janine. Janine was fascinated by Valerie. She got tongue-tied around her. Of course, she was only about twenty-five at the time. Both she and Brian gushed every time they got to host the Millers. And occasionally, Waylon and Johnny's parents, Ed and Elaine Frederickson, were guests too. I'd say those were the main people. Mostly other couples.

"Ed, Brian, and Simon went out fishing a time or two, but it wasn't Simon's thing. He did it to tell his friends in New York he'd been fishing in North Dakota. Ed probably invited Simon in the first place, so they'd give Johnny and Waylon business. He and Brian weren't too broken up when Simon quit joining them. They're die-hard fishermen."

"Did Valerie have any female friends?" Courtney asked.

"She and Izzy got together quite a bit. She has a lot of free time since Tyson and his dad, Finn, do most of the work on the farm. If Izzy had the chance, she would happily move to a city, but the farm has been in Finn's family for generations. He's not moving. Tyson feels the same way as his dad."

Courtney couldn't come up with any further questions to ask Honor except about the timing of the Millers' disappearance, and she should let Honor get back to work. Then she reminded herself she was actually the boss, not Honor, and she could do whatever she wanted.

"So, tell me about the time when the Millers disappeared. What season was it, if that helps you recall some information?" It happened in summer, but if it helped Honor bring up more details, she would coach her a little. "I know it was a long time ago."

"It was the Fourth of July weekend. With the fourth being on a Monday, some people probably took Tuesday off too. That sticks in my mind because the Millers were going to leave on the fifth. We told them it wasn't such a great idea because they'd never driven the RV very far. There would be lots of traffic the next day."

"Who else was there when you told them?" Courtney considered driving an RV in a lot of traffic and decided it wasn't something she wanted to do. The Millers must have been an adventurous couple.

"Oh, it's easy to remember. Valerie and Simon hosted a Fourth of July party the night before they left." Honor smiled at the memory.

"I'm surprised they did that the night before leaving early the next morning. Who wants to party before they take a long road trip?" Courtney couldn't imagine.

"They did. They dug a hole in the backyard." Honor shivered at the memory. Maybe she remembered someone else had dug a bunch of holes in the backyard not long ago. "Simon wanted to have all these fireworks. He was lucky it was a wet year, and we didn't have a burn ban going on at the time. He wanted to prop the fireworks in the hole and light them, which he did. It was a gorgeous display."

"And who was there that night?" Courtney remembered Doug talking about the hole and how they'd found the Millers' bodies there.

"Doug and I were there. Janine, Brian, Izzy, and Finn. It was a small group. Just right." She was quiet for a minute. "They also invited Ed and Elaine Frederickson, but they had something going on at home. Lori was only about ten years old then, so I suppose she might have been the reason. Simon and Valerie didn't drink much because of their trip the next day, but Brian and Doug didn't let that hold them back. I imagine Ed and Elaine knew how the night would go." She shook her head.

"The men did have a disagreement about something stupid. I don't know what it was about, except probably something to do with fishing. Or maybe I associate their argument with fishing because Brian and Doug were going out the next morning." She shrugged. "Maybe one of the others who was there would remember.

"Like I said, there was some family thing going on that must have carried into the next day. Or maybe Ed didn't want to go with Doug and Brian. Brian didn't usually go with them, and when he did, Ed usually found an excuse not to go. I don't think he likes Brian." Honor shrugged.

"Did you have a lot to do the next day, or did you get to celebrate with the men?" She smiled at Honor.

Honor gave a strained smile. "I don't care to drink too much, so I only had a glass of wine. Janine didn't drink much either, because we also had plans for the next day."

"I didn't realize you and Janine are friends." She had never seen the two really talking together. "I'm sorry. That sounded like criticism. I meant she seems to know her work as well as you know your job."

"Oh, Janine is very accomplished at construction. You'll be happy to see what she can do when we start getting to the painting and finishing touches. She's a genius." Honor's tone sounded a little jealous or almost like it was an insult.

"Good to know. We'll have a lot of finishing touches for everyone to do with this big building. I'm sure you do excellent work, as well as Janine." She prudently changed the direction of the conversation. "So, Janine and you were almost as sober as Valerie and Simon. How about Tyson's parents, Izzy and Finn? How were they around the Millers?"

"They were the most disappointed when Valerie and Simon announced they planned to move and sell their house. There's a hierarchy in a small town, like anywhere else." Honor was quiet for a moment. "I'd say Izzy and Finn are at the top. The Millers were up there with them while they lived here."

Courtney nearly smiled, as Honor took the bait. Nothing encouraged someone to keep talking as much as trying to defend themselves. Honor was at the party and knew quite a bit about the movements of Elm City residents the day the Millers went missing. Courtney's suspect list for the Millers' death was narrowing down to the couples who were at the party and also Tyson for Waylon's death.

"Yes. I can see how that would be. The idle rich among the middle-class farmers." Courtney made it sound worse than she meant.

Honor glared at her like she was not enjoying the conversation.

"That's not how it was." Honor jumped down from the tailgate. "I didn't mean to imply the Millers thought they were better than anyone else. In fact, they told some story of starting out poor and being lucky enough for Simon to get a great job in finance, which helped them become wealthy. They were very kind and normal with everyone in the community."

"I'm sorry," Courtney said. "They sound like they were a nice couple. And if they were anything like Gary, well, he seems like a good guy."

Honor settled down after those words and leaned back against the tailgate.

"So, to sum up: the group got together, and the next morning, the Millers' RV was gone as expected. Everyone believed they'd taken off on their move to Virginia as planned. Doug and Brad went out fishing early, and you and Janine stayed home and took care of the chores. Izzy and Finn also spent the following day at home. Do I have it right?"

"Not quite. Janine and I were a little peeved at the guys for taking off to fish and leaving us to languish at home working. We decided we'd go to Bismarck for a spa day." She laughed. "So, we disappeared before they were even up for their fishing trip, and let me tell you, that was early. But we got to Bismarck before traffic and had a great day, starting with a big breakfast someone else cooked."

She laughed again. "The men were royally mad at us when they returned from fishing because they were hungover and had to do chores before they could go. Janine and I still bring it up every once in a while when we want to remind them we aren't hired help."

Courtney laughed with her. "Brilliant idea."

"We thought so." Honor smiled at her.

"Well, thanks for the information. I hope the sheriff has some ideas soon."

"Will they get any evidence from those tools he took yesterday?" Honor asked.

Courtney shrugged. "I doubt it. Time will tell." She slid off the tailgate and landed by Honor. "I should go and let you get back to work."

Honor nodded. "Yep. Although this group is good at keeping on task, even when I'm not in sight. I do have to work on the project. I hope we get Johnny back."

"I do too. I'll let you know if I hear anything." Courtney went back to her vehicle. She felt in the way this morning, as Honor's crew worked on the first floor of the inn, and Luke's team shuffled around the roof. She was happy to see them using a lot of safety equipment. Her own fear of heights kept her feet on the ground.

She sat in the driver's seat and pulled out a legal tablet and pens to make notes after talking to Honor. She made two columns and started a list of possible suspects. She listed each couple together, as she was sure it would have taken two people to kill the Millers. One person drove the RV to South Dakota, and the other person followed to give him or her a ride back to Elm City. Eight years was a long time to get alibis from people, but maybe she could see if Gary had access to the police reports. She'd ask if there were any questions about where everyone was at the time his parents disappeared.

If Honor hadn't lied to her, Doug and Brian should have alibis for each other, and Janine and Honor had alibis together. However, that meant either the men could have killed the Millers, or Janine and Honor could have done it. She had a hard time seeing the women as killers.

Or all four were in on it. Or one of the couples did it and used the other couple for alibis, each couple thinking they could protect their friends and themselves. Or…she was starting to go in circles.

CHAPTER 26

Time to go visit Izzy and Finn, since they had been at the party that night. As promised, she texted Alex to say where she was going.

She took the same route she'd taken the other day and drove by Robb Bearman's farm on the way. She wanted to stop and see his miniature horses, but he was at the construction site, and she didn't want to let herself into his barn without his knowledge. She'd have to visit them some other time.

When she pulled into the long driveway of the Collins' farmstead, she was impressed by the large, manicured lawn in front of the farmhouse. Someone had great landscaping skills. Everything appeared to have grown there naturally in the perfect spot.

The hedge along one side of the lawn was perfectly trimmed. Purple, red, blue, yellow, and orange plants and flowers grew in a carefully configured circle with an angel fountain gracing the middle of the plants. She didn't want to pull up the driveway to talk with Izzy and Finn. She wanted to park along the driveway and admire the view. The white house and red barn and outbuildings completed the picture-perfect farm. She no longer questioned why Tyson wanted to continue the family legacy.

Ignoring the urge to park and gawk, she drove up the driveway and parked in front of the house. She hadn't even gotten out of the vehicle with the plate of cookies she'd brought before Izzy opened the front door. At least the fifty-something woman appeared to be Izzy. Her professionally cut hair fell along her sculpted cheekbones in a straight blond style complementing her blue eyes. "Hello."

"Hi." Once she reached the woman in jeans and a light blue t-shirt, she stretched out her hand. "Courtney Richmond. It's nice to meet you."

"You too." Izzy's handshake was firm. "Tyson likes working for you and your husband."

Courtney smiled. "Good to hear. He does a great job. You must be proud of him."

"Oh, yes. We're proud of all our children." She smiled sweetly. "Even the teenage troublemakers. Come on in."

"Tyson said he has some siblings."

"They're at school at the moment." Izzy led Courtney into a surprisingly comfortable living room.

Courtney handed her the plate of chocolate chip cookies she'd brought.

"Thank you, dear," Izzy said. "Would you like one?"

"No, thank you, but go ahead if you want one."

A few deer trophy heads at the far side of the room stopped her momentum before she continued following Izzy to a brown plaid couch. A glass center in the coffee table made Courtney shiver at how careful the kids had to be in the room. Izzy set the cookie plate on the table.

Her own brothers rough-housed too much to have anything glass within their vicinity. Two brown leather chairs with wool plaid throws were placed on each side of the coffee table facing it. A television was the focal point across from the couch and for the chairs. Obviously an important part of the décor. She'd expected something upscale and charming, but it was almost manly in atmosphere. The white walls covered in various floral paintings and family photos softened the room.

After her hostess's request to call her Izzy and an offer of a drink, which Courtney declined, they settled in each of the armchairs, the coffee table between them.

"Tyson told us you're renovating the Miller farm into an inn. Sounds like a big endeavor." Izzy smiled across the distance.

"Not as big as this farm." Courtney laughed. "It's gorgeous here. I wanted to park and stare at your lovely garden."

Izzy's eyes lit up. "It's my pride and joy. I've been in the garden club ever since I married Finn and moved here. I love to try new things. Usually, I put those plants in the backyard until I decide on their permanent home. I treat them better than my children."

"Well, they're beautiful, but I doubt you treat them better than your kids. Tyson speaks very highly of you."

A frown crossed her face. "He's smart. He could do anything, but he's fallen in love with farm life. Like his father." She sighed. "Oh, well. I'm happy if he's happy."

"I'm sure it must have been hard for you when the Millers decided to move. You and Valerie were friends."

Izzy nodded. "It was difficult when they decided to move. For a short time, I questioned if I was missing something in life, but my life is Finn and the children. Of course, they were in grade school back when the Millers were here. I have them and my garden. I'm happy. It's nice to talk to someone about Valerie. She was a terrific woman."

"I'm glad you had time with her." Courtney settled back on her seat. "Do you mind if I ask you about the Millers? I'm kind of interested in what happened to them, because we bought their house." Izzy said she enjoyed talking about Valerie, so Courtney stayed silent, waiting.

"Sure. It's not often I get to talk about them to anyone. They didn't exactly keep to themselves, but they were only in the area for two years. About the time we became closer friends, they moved. Or we believed they moved." She shrugged. "I guess now we know they didn't actually leave." Her eyes displayed a hint of sadness.

"That must have been a shock when they were discovered."

"Well, yes and no. I mean, when they disappeared, we all hoped for the best." Izzy made eye contact. "But underneath our hopes, we all knew something bad happened to them. It was a matter of time, although we didn't expect eight years to pass before something new would come to light."

Courtney nodded.

"And they were found in their own backyard." She shook her head. "I simply can't imagine who in our community killed them, and let me say, I really don't want to dwell on it too long. Unfortunately, Waylon is another victim, which changes everything."

Not sure what Izzy meant, she asked, "Why does Waylon's death change things?"

"What a surprise when we found out Waylon knew where the jewelry was all this time."

"But he left it in the ground all this time," Courtney said, puzzled.

"He gave them to Patty, and she gave them to the police. It doesn't take much to figure out what happened when the sheriff and Gary stopped at Patty's house. Afterward, they announced the jewels were found. And all this happened right after Waylon died."

Courtney had hoped people would put it together. They did. The police picking up the jewelry should keep Patty safe. They were now beyond anyone's reach. Also, no more digging done at her and Alex's inn by someone searching for them. "That's what I heard."

"Small town." Izzy shrugged and smiled.

Tired of the phrase, Courtney changed the subject. "Honor told me you and your husband were at the Millers' the night before they were going to leave."

"That's right. Finn and I went. Honor and Doug, and Brian and Janine were there too. The Frederiksons had other plans. It was a good number. Half of us drank; the other half didn't, so no one was left out. I wondered how Brian and Doug could get up early and fish considering their alcohol consumption, but they're younger than me." As if considering the folly of the young, she shook her head. "Janine and Honor had a glass each."

"You have a good memory."

"It's mostly clear in my head. Mainly because the women usually joined their husbands while drinking, although Janine often stayed sober. She has a sensible view of not driving after drinking. Now they have children, she's extra careful. But back to that night… Valerie and Simon abstained because of their early morning drive. Brian and Doug were the drinkers, and they almost created a fire in the backyard when Simon was setting off fireworks.

"He'd dug a hole just deep enough to put some fireworks into it. They were supposed to be held in the little square hole in the dirt, and he'd light them and step away. It should have been safe, but Brian got the idea to see how many fireworks they could put in the hole at one time, and he lit it on fire.

"Unlike when Simon carefully positioned the ones he shot off, Brian's pile shot off in all directions, and we actually had to duck because one came right toward us. The guys went around the whole outside of the house, making sure they hadn't started a fire with the low-shooting fireworks." She shook her head.

"Other than that incident, did anything odd happen?" Courtney heard about the fireworks three times. She wanted new information.

"No. And believe me, once those people from Virginia called the sheriff's office and said they couldn't reach the Millers, and they hadn't taken possession of the house, we were all reconsidering the events. But everything seemed normal. And the next days and weeks—well, nothing happened. Not one thing sticks out in my mind." She shivered. "But now with Waylon's death, I'm afraid."

Courtney nodded. "It's scary someone is capable of that kind of behavior."

"It is. I tell my children to be extra careful, and I admit, I've become an overly protective mom. I want to know where they're at all the time now. Trust me when I say it's hard enough to have your teenagers stay in contact. They aren't handling the situation gracefully."

"That's understandable, but I bet you're tired of fighting them. Hopefully, the sheriff will have some answers soon." Courtney tried to reassure her.

"I'm guessing you're doing a little looking around yourself." Izzy's eyes twinkled despite her somber expression.

"Me? No. I wanted to meet people in the area, and since Tyson works for us, I decided I'd visit you."

"Right." Izzy's eyes still twinkled, and a smile overtook her face.

Courtney couldn't resist her charm and smiled back. She hoped she wasn't considering Izzy innocent because of her personality.

Izzy contemplated the plate of cookies on the coffee table. "One thing has changed in the past few years, and that's Janine and Brian's relationship. I'm not saying it has anything to do with what happened with the Millers. It's something I've noticed."

"What's happening?"

"Janine acts timid. And sometimes I think it *is* an act. She has this sly smile sometimes, like she's playing a part. Oh, dear." She was silent, then considered Courtney for a moment. "I admit I'm not a fan of Janine's. I'm not sure why she annoys me. She used to be rather adventurous and up for any kind of fun time."

Izzy raised her hands and let them fall on her lap. "It could be the normal growth of their marriage. Now they have children, and Janine wants to do it right. She grew up in a poor family with only her mother. She and Brian aren't loaded, but they're comfortable."

Courtney nodded. "I see. You're right. It could mean something or nothing. Maybe I'll try and catch Janine at home when Brian's at work. I happen to know their schedule."

"Brian used to expect the Millers to pay for everything whenever we went out to eat or an event. It got to be rather embarrassing. I'm not saying he stole those jewels, and somehow Waylon came to have them in his possession. But I wouldn't put it past him either."

"Thanks." Courtney stood up. "You've been a font of information."

The twinkle came back to Izzy's eyes. "Right. But you're not investigating."

CHAPTER 27

Courtney called Gary and invited him to visit Janine with her. They took her truck. "You have the day off?"

"Yes. I'm a little tired of working one county over. When are you going to solve what happened to my parents so I can come back?" He laughed at her expression.

Her mouth hung open, and she closed it with a snap. "Funny. You've had a lot longer than I have to figure it all out. Give me a few more days." She glanced at him. "How are you doing?"

"Okay, I guess. It's rather strange knowing where my parents are and what happened to them." He stared out the windshield. "I wish I knew more."

"You'll be happy to learn what I've found out. How about coming for grilled steak and vegetables? The evening is too dark to sit outside, but Alex will cook everything on the grill, and we'll eat in the kitchen. This might be our last good day to use the grill. What do you say? We can talk about everything and pool results."

She had turned onto the Langs' driveway.

"Wow. They don't seem to be hurting for money. I've never had to come out this way." He gazed around at the well-kept buildings. "One or both of them keep this place looking good. Most of the farms I've seen are run-down, and the owners are one step from moving to the city to find work."

Courtney parked in front of the house where she'd parked her first visit. "I agree. In fact, I believed every farm must be this neat around here. Now, I believe it's the company your parents kept. Maybe they were drawn to certain personalities."

"My parents didn't scold me for leaving my things lying around when I was growing up." Gary's memories seemed to make him happy. "Our house was usually clean, and things were in their place most of the time. It was normal for me. Probably why I did okay in the Air Force. Everything has a place there."

"I bet." What experiences had shaped Gary in the Air Force? Now wasn't the time to ask.

Maybe he'd never share information about his time in the service.

They got out of the vehicle and were greeted once again by the collies, who ran back and forth between her and Gary. There were also children playing quietly in the yard.

Janine came outside and said something to the kids Courtney couldn't hear over the barking of the dogs. The kids nodded instant agreement, which struck Courtney as odd. Most kids whined whenever told to do something. Janine came over to them. "Hi. It's nice to see you, Courtney. And you too, Gary." She glanced at Courtney.

"He was free, and I have a few more questions you can answer. I talked to Honor this morning."

Janine's eyes dropped to the ground. "She told me. Are you sure you want to talk about this?" She peeked up at Gary.

"Definitely. You can say anything. I only want the truth," he assured her.

There was a picnic table on the lawn on the opposite side of the driveway from where the children played. Janine led her and Gary to it, and they all sat down. Once more, Courtney noticed Janine biting on her nail.

She quickly pulled it out of her mouth when she saw Courtney notice. "So. What can I tell you? Honor said you asked about the night and next day when Gary's parents left. Or were supposed to leave." Her face turned red.

"Hey," Gary said, "don't worry about it. Pretend I never met them, if that helps."

She threw a grateful look at him. "We had a get-together for the Fourth of July. We went to the your parents' house about eight or nine in the evening. We had plenty of time to eat and have some drinks before it got dark enough to shoot off the fireworks. Simon was as giddy as a child. He was so excited about the system he'd set up in the backyard." She smiled wistfully at the memory.

"He'd dug a hole the right size so the fireworks would stand up straight, and he hoped they'd shoot straight up into the sky. It worked most of the time. Brian and Doug had a lot to drink, and they convinced Simon to give them several of the fireworks. After making the hole bigger, they stuffed them all inside at the same time." She shook her head.

Courtney had just heard this story from Izzy. They matched on details.

"Sounds like a dumb thing to do," Gary said. "Forgive me for my bluntness."

Janine nodded and smiled. "The rest of us agreed, but Brian moved fast. The guys lit them before we could say much, and there was a lot of running to get out of the way." She started giggling. "Thinking of it now, we must have appeared ridiculous. Idiots."

Courtney wasn't sure if there was a hint of dislike mixed in with the softer look on Janine's face.

"So, the guys were drinking. How about the rest of you?" Gary asked.

"Not as much. A glass or two over the evening. It was dark around ten. We left around 11:30 or midnight. There was no reason to check the time, so we weren't paying attention. No kids yet." She glanced over at the three children playing. "We shot off the fireworks, said a few more things and left."

"Who left first?"

Janine considered her answer. "No one, really. We were all tired. Once Izzy and Finn said they needed to get home and mentioned Valerie and Simon had to get on the road early, that was it. We hugged them goodbye, and all of us left." She smiled slightly. "I remember thinking we were making a sort of train as we all drove down the gravel road one after another until we each turned off in the direction of our own farms."

"And the next day?" Gary asked.

"Someone reported their RV was gone, and we all assumed they were on the road." Janine reached to put her finger in her mouth but stopped midway and dropped her hand on the picnic table.

One of the kids yelled something to her about being hungry. She pointed at the house, and they all ran inside. Courtney assumed there was a snack waiting for them.

"I only have a few more minutes before one of them has a meltdown." She smiled softly.

"The plight of parenthood," Courtney said.

"Exactly."

"What did you do the day after the party?" She waited for Janine's response.

Her face set in a frown. "Honor and I went to Bismarck to have a spa day. Honor wanted to pay back the guys for getting stinking drunk. As soon as we were both home after the party at Valerie and Simon's house, she texted me and said we should get up early and go before the guys went fishing. She didn't want to do the chores while the guys got to fish all day.

"I wasn't thrilled with the idea. We didn't get much sleep, and I was tired. But making Brian do the chores appealed to me, so I went." She shrugged.

"What time did they go fishing?" Gary had a stillness about him as he sat there absorbing the information. Fully dialed into the conversation.

"They were supposed to leave at 6:00 a.m., but I'm guessing it was closer to 7:00 or 7:30 a.m. when they managed to leave. Depending on how sick they felt when they got up and how fast they moved." She shrugged again. It seemed she didn't care.

"Wow. So, you and Honor must have left around 5:30 a.m. You must have been tired. That isn't much sleep."

Janine smiled. "Honor was determined to get back at them. She drove, knowing if I'd offered to drive, I wouldn't have shown up at her house. I would have gone back to sleep. On purpose. But she pulled into the driveway right on time."

"Sounds like she had a grievance against Doug," Gary suggested.

"She hated all the drinking he did."

"Yet they're still married. They don't appear to get along." Would Janine volunteer any information?

"They're both eager to start their own construction company. They need each other to get out of this town. Neither can do it on their own. I don't understand how Honor puts up with Doug's frowning face every day."

A shiver slid down Courtney's arms. She and Alex loved each other. If the inn didn't happen, she wouldn't blame him. He wouldn't blame her. She also couldn't imagine getting back at him for the times he'd wronged her. Not in such a blatant way. Yes, she got angry at him. She'd likely make him get his own meal and eat without him, but to plan a revenge scene? Nope. She didn't understand. But Alex wasn't a drinker, so she shouldn't be judgy.

"Makes sense," Courtney said. "Any idea how Waylon ended up with the jewels? He doesn't seem to be part of the group Gary's parents socialized with."

Janine frowned and shook her head. "It's a mystery to me. He did some work on their house, but he worked on everyone's house around here at one time or another. I never saw them together socially."

Had Gary's parents decided to move because the only person they trusted was the local plumber, who was a nice guy?

Gary stood up, and Courtney followed him to the truck. "We'll get out of your way."

Janine laughed. "I need to go check on the little ones. I'm surprised one of them hasn't run out here complaining about another one hitting them. Then again, quiet is scary too. They could be into anything."

Courtney noticed the circles under Janine's eyes. Maybe the conversation had been more nerve-racking than Janine wanted to admit. Her laugh seemed strained.

"Thanks for the information," Courtney said.

As they drove out of the yard, Gary said, "That's one stressed-out woman."

She sent him a quick glance before returning to the view in front of her. "Yes. She's not as good at lying as Honor, but which part did she lie about? What do you think?"

"They didn't go to Bismarck to a spa."

CHAPTER 28

Shock reverberated through Courtney at his words. "Why don't you believe Honor and Janine went to the spa?"

"When does Alex get home?" he asked instead of answering her.

"Whenever I call him." She laughed tightly. It sounded like he was at her beck and call, but she could tell Gary wanted to talk to both of them at the same time and soon. "Actually, in a few hours. Let's go to the construction site. I should put in an appearance. Then I can have a conversation with Doug, and we can come home and talk. He can leave early."

Gary agreed, and when they reached the inn, they parked on the far side with the other vehicles. There were still men on the roof but less debris falling to the ground. They both put on their hard hats and went inside.

Courtney said hello to Alex. "Gary and I are going to talk to Doug, and then do you want to come home and start some food on the grill?"

He looked around at the other workers. Honor stood talking to Robb, and their conversation appeared serious. Courtney joined them. "Is something wrong?"

They glanced up in surprise. "No. The usual construction issues," Honor assured her.

Robb smiled and nodded. "Yep. Normal stuff."

"Okay. Just getting concerned because we haven't had any problems lately."

Robb laughed. "Be happy for these days. Sometime we'll be contacting you with an issue, and you'll have time to worry. Don't buy trouble."

"Right." Brian and Gary were talking. She left them alone, not wanting to interrupt Gary's conversation. He'd tell them about it later.

Spotting Doug, she headed in his direction, leaving Honor and Robb to finish their conversation. She invited Doug to join her outside, and he followed her without asking any questions. He must have spoken to Honor about Courtney's talk with her earlier.

She perched on the end of one of the tailgates again. Doug stood a few feet away, staring into the distance.

"What can I help you with?" he asked impatiently. "I'm right in the middle of measurements for the kitchenette, and I want to finish before the end of the day."

"This will only take a few minutes." She decided to go right for the details. Doug wasn't going to have a long talk with her. "Did you and Brian go fishing the day after the party at the Millers' on July Fourth?"

His face morphed into astonishment. Maybe Honor hadn't talked to him. Or what else had he expected her to ask him?

"You're asking if we went fishing eight or nine years ago?" He started pacing.

"It's not a hard question. A couple disappeared. I'm sure everyone replayed what they were doing when that happened. And you don't look senile."

He let out a brief laugh but kept pacing. "Of course, we all remember, but I don't see what it has to do with you." He hadn't seen Gary come out of the building behind him.

Courtney had.

Gary raised his eyebrows and tilted his head. "It has a lot to do with me."

Doug swung around in surprise. "Gary."

"Right. Did you go fishing with someone the day after the party?"

"Yes. Brian and I went. I'm sure Honor and Janine told you about the trick they played on us. It makes a great story." He stood there staring between the two of them. "Is that it?"

"Not quite." Gary glanced over at the road that passed the driveway into the inn.

Courtney heard a vehicle and looked in the same direction. The sheriff's SUV.

Sheriff Warren drove, and there was a deputy in the passenger seat. What did they want? Something to do with one of the murders, of course. Her heart raced, and her palms started sweating. She noticed Gary squinting at them in concentration. Doug stood unnaturally still after his earlier restlessness.

The sheriff and deputy got out of the black SUV and walked in unison to where the three of them were talking.

"Doug Bellis." He stepped closer to Doug and pulled out his handcuffs. "Please turn around and place your hands on the top of the tailgate here." He pointed to a pickup two away from Courtney's position and started reading Doug his rights.

Doug's face showed his shock as he followed directions. Gone was the smirk and the smart attitude. "Um…"

"You're under arrest for suspicion of murder of Waylon Frederickson."

"I haven't murdered anyone." He removed his hands from the truck and backed away.

"Stop right there." The sheriff put his hand on the butt of his gun. "Move back to the truck and put your hands on the tailgate."

Doug stood still for a moment, his wide eyes terrified. Then he followed the sheriff's instructions.

The sheriff continued with the rest of the legalese and put the cuffs on Doug. Without a word to Courtney or Gary, they led their prisoner to the county vehicle and took off.

Courtney slid off the tailgate. "Did they find some evidence with those screwdrivers?"

"Something led to Doug." Gary shook his head. "I'm not convinced he's guilty."

"Okay. Let's do him a favor. We'll tell Honor he's been arrested, so she can find an attorney. I don't care if he's guilty at this point. Innocent until proven guilty." Courtney thought of Alex taking the blame for Steven for a crime he didn't commit.

Gary didn't reply.

"I'll be back shortly with Alex and Honor. Honor can take care of Doug, and you can come home with Alex and myself for a discussion of this whole case. I haven't told you both everything I've learned."

Gary remained outside, while Courtney went to get the other two. She gestured from the front door for them to come outside, pointing to the vehicle driving down the road. "The sheriff came and arrested Doug. I'm sorry," she said to Honor.

Honor's face remained a remote mask. "I'll take care of this. What did they charge him with?"

"Suspicion of murder of Waylon Frederickson," Courtney said softly. Honor's stillness was unsettling.

A frown crossed Honor's face. "Can Robb close up tonight and deal with Luke's staff's questions? He's capable."

"Definitely," Courtney told her.

"I'll talk to him and then get Doug a lawyer." Honor disappeared back inside, and Alex followed Courtney over to Gary.

"Let's get going," Gary said. "I don't want to see Honor right now. I'll ride with Alex."

Courtney nodded before they hurried to the vehicles and took off into town. She pulled up to the garage, and Alex parked on the street. Gary's face remained shuttered, and Alex shrugged when Courtney looked at him.

When they got into the house, Courtney guided Gary to the recliner. "Have a chair and continue pondering."

He smiled faintly and sat down where she suggested.

"Alex and I will get us all something to eat and drink." She went out and started the grill.

When she entered the kitchen, Alex had the steak and vegetables out of the fridge. "I left the lemonade for you to make. Let's have pink lemonade."

She poked her head around the corner to the living room. "Do you like pink lemonade?"

"Do you mind if I have coffee?" he asked.

"No problem. What kind?"

"Black, no cream or sugar."

She nodded and went back to the kitchen. "You still want lemonade? Gary's having coffee."

"I'm thirsty. Lemonade would be perfect. I'll have some decaf coffee later." He'd already cut the vegetables and put the cubes on skewers. The steaks were seasoned. While he went outside to put them all on the grill, she made Gary's coffee.

She finished making the lemonade and joined Gary in the living room with his coffee and her lemonade. After handing him his cup, she sat on the couch. "Come to any conclusions?"

"I'm getting there." He took a sip of coffee and leaned back against the recliner. "I'm finally going to have the answer to my parents' last hours, and we'll all know what happened to Waylon. I might not have mentioned him, but he's as much in my thoughts as my parents since he was killed."

"If he had told the police about the jewels sooner, would he be alive today?" Courtney sipped her lemonade.

"Maybe. Maybe not. He might have come across something else he didn't tell anyone." Gary took another sip of his coffee and leaned forward. "Should I go out and help Alex?"

"No. He needs a little time alone. He's not used to being around so many people all day long. I'm starting to regret being absent from the building site, and he's been good enough to let me go my own way." Alex loved her, but he was helping her with her dream inn while she ran around the countryside. "I need to get to the construction site tomorrow and let him stay home for a while."

"He loves you and doesn't care if you're there or not." Gary frowned. "I'm jealous of not having someone in my life who cares about me like that. I've been too busy trying to figure out what happened with my parents."

"Maybe we'll know soon. Since they arrested Doug for Waylon's murder, they must have evidence."

"They do. But did he kill my parents too?"

"You have someone in the department keeping you informed. Right?" Courtney laughed as his face turned red. "I knew it."

"Well, let's say I made a deal with him, and, no, I'm not telling you who it is. When they arrest someone for my parents' death, he'll call me, and I'll be at the interview," he said grimly.

"Behind the glass, right? They won't let you be in on the questioning."

"No way. That would put the case in jeopardy, and as much as I want to interview the person who got away so long with murder, I don't want to ruin the chance of them being found guilty and going to prison."

"If Doug is guilty, that will relieve Alex's mind about me being at the construction site. You'll also have your answers when they question him."

"My friend is keeping a close watch for me."

"It's time for Johnny to come home, or at least tell us what Waylon said to him." Courtney took a sip of her drink.

"You know where he's at?" Gary asked.

"I do. But I promised to keep it a secret. It's up to his family and Johnny to share that information. Not me. But they might let me go see him if I ask nicely." She fluttered her eyelashes, something she didn't have a lot of practice doing.

"I'll be my usual charming self and convince them we need some information. Since I'm not law enforcement, and no one seems to be planning to arrest him—because they've arrested Doug—they'll be okay with me talking to him for a short time. I hope."

"I can see where Johnny needed to get away after Waylon's death. I hope he doesn't fall apart without his brother." Gary cared about Johnny's well-being.

Courtney found his attitude refreshing. So many people saw Johnny as the town drunk and not a person. "Yes. Death of a loved one is hard, but I imagine you're as aware of that fact as Johnny. He's grieving, but maybe he can help us with Doug's part in what happened to Waylon. However, there's always the chance Waylon took the answers to his grave…"

CHAPTER 29

After Alex cooked everything on the grill, they gathered at the kitchen table to eat. The darkness outside descended at around six, and it was half past the hour when they were ready to sit down.

After Alex said the prayer of thanks, talk turned back to Doug's arrest. "We need to go through your list after we're finished eating," he said to Courtney.

At Gary's puzzled look, Courtney enlightened him. "I've made a list of suspects and possible motives and alibis. The alibis column is slim because it was so long ago."

"Great. We'll compare notes." Gary took another bite of his steak. When he'd finished swallowing, he grinned at Alex. "Want to be my chef? I hate cooking."

He shook his head. "I'm only good at the grill."

"He's being modest. He does most of the cooking," Courtney told Gary. "Or we cook together."

Gary nodded.

When they'd finished eating and cleaned the kitchen, Alex got himself and Gary a cup of coffee, and the three of them settled in the living room.

Courtney had her notes on her lap, but she ignored them at first. "What happened with the screwdriver testing and the jewel testing?"

"You're a woman with a dream to build an inn to help people. What's with all the questions and investigating you've been doing?" He seemed more curious than upset.

Courtney glanced at Alex, and he nodded. She turned back to Gary. "We told you what we want to do with the inn. One week a month we want our guests to stay the whole week and get spiritual and psychological counseling, along with time to spend alone figuring out the next steps in their life. Or to make a decision if there's some big event going on in their life."

"Right," Gary said. "I remember."

"Well, the thing is, Alex and I are the only ones here in Elm City who know the whole plan. Everyone else thinks we're going to have a regular inn."

"What does that have to do with anything?"

Courtney smiled at his confusion. "Imagine the surprise Alex and I had when we got a call from our co-owners in Bismarck, who will be joining us to run the inn once it's ready. Someone donated a substantial amount of money to help us get the inn going. They told us it was an anonymous donor."

"Terrific. I hope it helps, but again, what does that have to do with me?" His confusion gave way to a cautious glance between her and Alex.

"As you're well aware by now, I'm curious by nature. Only a few people could have donated, and one of them was you. Of course, I looked up the price you sold the Virginia house for, and guess what I found."

Gary's face settled into a satisfied smile. "Courtney, I believe your skills will be wasted as an inn owner, although your inn plans are noble. Yes, you'd make a better investigator."

"I'll check out getting a P.I. license when the inn is ready. You okay with that?" she asked Alex.

"Go for it." He put his arm around her shoulders and drew her closer to him on the couch.

They both stared at Gary. "Thank you for the donation," they said in unison and laughed.

"You didn't expect anything from us," Courtney said. "That was incredibly generous."

"I didn't want you to find out." He shrugged. "I didn't count on you being the Agatha Christie of the village."

"We appreciate it, so we're helping. Also, we're aware it might be hard for you to get information from other law enforcement, even if you have an inside source. We want you to get answers, and we would help even if you hadn't donated to our cause. Thank you."

"You're welcome. Now, can we move on to the suspect list? I'm not comfortable with all this thanks, but I do appreciate it. And you'll both do a marvelous job with your guests." Gary shuffled around on the recliner, trying to get comfortable.

"Sure. One more thing," Courtney said. "Relax. We've decided to name our new venture

Crocus Hill Inn. Remember the day in the spring when you showed us the house for the first time? Along the whole long driveway on the side of the road opposite the house were all those crocuses. We decided since they're a spring flower and show new life is on the way, it would be a good name."

Gary nodded. "Excellent. My parents would love the name. It's better than what I keep hearing. The Millers' house. Now I can replace it in my head with Crocus Hill Inn."

"You're the first person we've told. Other than the brand designer and our co-owners."

"I'm honored. Thank you."

"Okay." Courtney pulled her papers toward her. "Let's move on so you can relax. I've written down some things that stood out for me with everyone I've talked to. Let's see if anything means something to either of you. But first, anything on the screwdrivers or jewels?"

"This is among us," Gary said. "Sheriff Warren has been kind enough to share information on Waylon's murder. We're both pretending it doesn't have anything to do with my parents' death, so we can get away with him telling me.

Doug's arrest happened because his screwdriver came back with his prints and Waylon's blood on it."

"Oh, wow. I can see why he was arrested. That's pretty convincing." Courtney looked down at her papers. "Did Doug and Brian really go fishing the day of your parents' disappearance? Or did they ride to the house together? One of them drove the RV, and the other followed in the vehicle they took over there. They pushed the RV into the ravine and came back with their fishing alibi."

Gary nodded. "It's a good guess with no evidence either way. Honor and Janine wouldn't have passed by the house on their way to Bismarck, so they wouldn't know if the RV was still there that early. They assumed the guys went fishing, didn't catch anything, and were home before Honor and Janine returned."

"It works," Alex agreed but didn't sound convinced. "There are a few other options."

Courtney's brows lifted. "Such as?"

"Gary, did the jewels have any fingerprints on them?"

"Waylon's and Patty's on the outside of the box. On the jewels, my mother's prints, and a few pieces had my dad's prints on them. The police matched them to the prints they'd collected from inside my parents' RV. Otherwise, nothing."

"No one else had a chance, according to what Waylon told Patty. Your mother told Waylon where she hid the jewels, in case something happened to them, and they weren't able to retrieve them." Alex paused to take a sip of coffee.

Courtney didn't add that his mother must have been thinking about him. He didn't need to hear about his mother's fear she might die.

"Waylon dug up the jewels when the structural crew left the construction site one night and gave the jewels to Patty to hold in her safe. She didn't tell anyone and only opened the box to look but not touch. Then Waylon was murdered, and she knew it was time to tell you and the police." Alex took another longer drink of his coffee and set the cup on the end table.

"Right," Gary said.

"Alex, what's your other theory about why someone would kill Gary's parents?" She noticed

Gary was as interested in Alex's theory as she was. And Alex hadn't been digging for answers.

CHAPTER 30

Alex's smug expression morphed into serious. "It's possible we at least have the killers among those four people: Doug, Brian, Honor, and Janine."

"What? Honor or Janine?" Courtney shook her head. "I can see Honor as a killer, but Janine? No way."

"You've spent more time with her than I have, but that's not what I was going to suggest. What if Brian and Janine stayed home that day? Honor and Doug told them some story about how they had to get something done. When Gary's parents disappeared, they asked Brian and Janine to lie for them. Doug asked Brian to confirm the fishing story, and Honor asked Janine to corroborate their trip to Bismarck."

"So, you're saying Honor and Doug went to steal the jewels and killed my parents?" Gary considered the scenario.

They all sat quietly digesting this new possibility.

"I can see Honor forcing Doug, or him going along with it all. And Honor would lead the others into her plan for alibis." Maybe Honor came up with the idea after seeing Valerie's emeralds. She wanted money for her construction company. What better way than to steal the jewels from Valerie to fund the company? Maybe murder wasn't part of the plan.

"Doug is pretty laid-back at the construction site," Alex contributed. "It takes him twice as long as anyone else to get things done—including me, and I have little to no construction experience. I can't see him planning and getting away with this."

"Because Honor ran the show," Gary echoed Courtney's deduction. "She's your forewoman, right? Everyone says she gets things done. All Doug would have had to do was lie and say he went fishing. Brian would certainly back him up, because that gives him an alibi too."

"But what if someone said they didn't see them fishing?" Courtney asked.

"They say they went to some out-of-the-way place because of their late night, and they didn't want to deal with other fishermen. Plus, July fifth was a Tuesday. Lots of families probably had plans or worked. So, Doug asks Brian if he and Janine have an alibi, and they say no.

"Doug suggests the fishing story. Honor convinces Janine to lie and say they went to Bismarck for a spa day. All is taken care of," Alex finished the scene.

"Well, it sounds good." Courtney stared down at her papers. "But what about Waylon? Did he tell Johnny about the jewels or not? And Tyson was with Johnny that night. Did he know? How would Doug, Honor, Janine or Brian find out? Waylon and your parents were killed by the same person. I can't see two people in this small town as killers."

"You don't want to see more people as killers." Alex pulled her closer for a hug. "But I agree. I'm guessing it has to do with the jewels, and a lot of people were aware."

"Because Honor was sure to take the picture of Valerie wearing the emeralds and showed the picture to everyone she could. And she pretended to be ashamed of letting so many people see it." Gary started to sound ticked off. "We have our ringleader and one killer, but what about the second person in her scheme? Was it maybe Waylon—and then Honor killed him because he saw me around town and developed a conscience?"

Remembering the way Waylon always pulled out Patty's chair for her, Courtney shook her head. "I doubt Waylon was part of any murder. He knew where the jewels were and left them there eight years. Plus, he didn't have the personality to kill someone. His guilt would have gotten to him, and he would have confessed."

"I hate to say this, because you're probably right about Waylon, but there are lots of nice people who kill." Gary sounded sure.

"Okay, I bow to your knowledge on that score. But Waylon left the jewels in place, waiting until he had an idea what to do with them. When Alex and I started renovating the inn, he started thinking he should dig them up and give them to the seller. You," Courtney theorized.

"Right."

"That's what Waylon waited for. Plus, he was probably afraid someone would accuse him of murdering your parents, but he trusted you. Once he decided, he gave them to Patty to hold. Probably because he didn't want anyone accidentally finding them at his place—he didn't have a safe. Am I right about the safe?"

"Right again."

"Guys without guns or lots of money don't need one. Before he dug up the jewels, he didn't have anything worth putting in a safe. He knew Patty had one, though, so he had her keep them. He trusted her with the secret. He told Johnny the morning of his death that he had them, and you were next on his list to inform. He was going to hand them over to you, but before he could, somehow Doug found out. Maybe Johnny told someone, who told Doug or Honor. If we go back to the idea they did it together."

"Maybe." Gary shoved his hand over the top of his head. "One thing seems wrong with that scenario. Knowing Johnny the way he did, wouldn't Waylon have given the jewels to me and then told Johnny?"

"That would have been the smart thing to do, but they were twins. He probably told Johnny first to be fair, because Waylon felt guilty keeping the knowledge to himself all those years. It was his way of making peace with Johnny, even if Johnny didn't know about any of it."

"I guess we're not going to know, unless Johnny can tell us," Courtney said. "I still need to convince Ed to let me go see Johnny. He's had almost a week to get himself somewhat together."

"So, a few more days of waiting shouldn't matter," Gary said.

At Courtney's protest, he said, "I'm as anxious as you are."

Courtney remembered Gary had been waiting for years for answers and reined in her curiosity. "Right." She looked at her papers again. "What do we think about Tyson killing Waylon over something to do with Lori and framing Doug? He could have taken Doug's screwdriver, used it to kill Waylon, and put it back where he got it."

The guys were shaking their heads.

Courtney sighed. "Tyson is no killer."

"I have to agree, honey," Alex said. "I don't see him leaving a screwdriver he used to kill Waylon where the police could find it or framing Doug. I'm leaning toward Honor being the ringleader years ago and convincing Doug to help steal the jewels. She might have found out Waylon had them. She could have grabbed Doug's screwdriver and used it."

"And framed him," Gary said grimly, his mouth tight after the words left his lips. "That makes her incredibly dangerous."

Alex nodded. "She's tired of Doug and wants to get rid of him. Get the jewels and frame Doug. Move out of town and have her construction company."

"We have no proof she's done anything wrong?" Courtney asked them.

The men nodded.

"But I think we're right," Courtney said. "Janine bites her nails whenever she's around someone asking questions. She's guilty of lying to the police or something else. She and Brian accepted Honor's suggestion they give each other alibis. She didn't go to Bismarck with Honor because Honor was busy with Doug. It's all speculation. She's afraid of Honor."

"If Honor framed Doug, I'd be afraid of her too," Alex said, shuddering.

"Janine was friendly when we were alone, but the minute he came in the room, she hardly spoke." Courtney knew the men would want facts. "Brian acted a bit strange too. Whenever Janine corrected him, he seemed ashamed or embarrassed. The dynamic between those two is weird."

"We need proof," Alex said. "Did you have anybody else on your list of suspects?"

"I doubt Izzy and Finn had anything to do with anyone's death. You've both almost convinced me to take Tyson off the list for Waylon's death. He would have been the perfect one to hear about the jewels from Johnny when they were out drinking that night," Courtney said.

"Right about the jewels, but he was only seventeen when my parents were killed, and I can't see a teenager helping someone else without bragging or some other slip about what he'd done. Look at the way he drives his red truck. He can't help himself, and he's twenty-five now. He couldn't have kept his part in the death a secret eight years ago," Gary said.

"Okay. He doesn't have a motive either. The jewels wouldn't have mattered to him. He had everything he needed from his family. He's at the bottom of the list," Courtney agreed. "I don't see anyone else capable. I know," she said to Gary. "Looks can be deceiving."

He smiled at her. "Right. Anyway, you've got it nailed down. Honor's the ringleader, and likely Doug helped. They probably offered some of the money from the jewelry sale to the Langs." He laughed. "But no one got the jewels. At least I can marvel no one made a cent off my parents' death, no matter who's guilty."

"Now, how do we prove it?" Courtney asked.

CHAPTER 31

Courtney, Alex, and Gary had moved to the kitchen table for a late evening snack. Gary studied Courtney's notes of her interviews with everyone. "These are good. You really should consider some kind of detective work."

Courtney laughed. "I'm building a dream inn to help people."

"Exactly. You can excavate their lives and help them put everything back together. It suits you," Gary said.

"Thanks. I hope you're right." She wanted the Crocus Hill Inn to be successful, but right now, she had more pressing issues. "Are you doing okay with all our talk this evening? You've seemed okay, but it must be hard to talk about all this."

He shook his head. "Tonight has been a relief. Different scenarios have tumbled around my head for years with no answers. We're coming close to solving everything. We need to find the weak link in that foursome and get someone to talk.”

“Janine,” Alex and Courtney said at the same time.

“Tell the sheriff what we think, and I’ll bet he can break Honor and Doug’s alibis,” Alex said.

“I’m thinking of starting with Brian,” Gary said. “We haven’t spent much time with him at all. What if their farm isn’t doing well, and they could use the funds? Maybe he framed Doug after he went too far and killed Waylon? Maybe he tried to convince Waylon to tell him where the jewels were, and it got out of hand.”

“Before talking to Brian, we need to ask Johnny what happened before he left town. We only talked to him about Waylon’s death. We didn’t ask him much, but he did say Waylon had texted him to come over so they could continue their discussion about something.”

“He did? I don’t remember,” Alex said.

“You were probably still at Waylon’s with the sheriff and Gary. That was before you all came back here and took Johnny home.”

“Okay. We have a plan. Courtney’s going to Ed and Elaine’s tomorrow to see if she can speak with Johnny. She'll find out what she can. Once Johnny tells us his story, we'll go and talk to Brian." Gary looked at Alex. "Okay with you?"

"Definitely. We'll put Robb in charge of the workers when Honor's busy with Doug's legal troubles, and I'll be there to mediate. Although, Robb has great people skills and knows how to direct the construction team. I don't expect any trouble."

Shortly after that, Gary left, but not before he asked Courtney to promise she'd be careful. She agreed and told him she'd call him when she was done talking to Johnny. She didn't plan to take no for an answer from Ed about visiting Johnny.

***

After Gary left, Alex settled on the couch. Courtney curled up beside him.

"Are you feeling left out?" she asked.

"What?" His mind had obviously been far away.

"Are you upset because Gary and I are asking people questions, and you've spent most of the time at the construction site?" she repeated.

"No." He hugged her closer.

She loved being near him and being held in his arms. She laid her head on his chest. "What were you thinking about?"

"Surprisingly, the day Gary showed us the inn. I remember coming up the driveway, the house on one side, the field of crocus blooms covering the ground on the other side of the road. Being with you made it twice as wonderful. We'd come home. It was our place."

She couldn't help the tears filling her eyes. "It was like coming home after everything we'd gone through. You were out of jail. We were starting over with my dream inn, and I was blessed to have a willing partner in you."

They sat there enjoying the memory.

Eventually, she moved, hating to disrupt the peace with ugliness. "We never expected to help Gary with anything more than a few questions so he could solve his parents' disappearance."

He shook his head. "We can't say Gary didn't ask us to help investigate when we bought the house. He told us everything he knew. And he warned us to quit if it got dangerous.”

“He did. I guess I wasn’t ready for the reality of what that meant. Especially Waylon’s murder. Do you think that’s why he donated to our inn?”

“Nope. He sees your vision of helping people, and he wanted his parents to have a legacy of sorts. This was his way of using some of his parents’ money to help others.”

“You sound certain.” Courtney looked at his face. His sweet brown eyes brimmed with tenderness as he stared back at her.

“I’m certain,” he whispered. The kiss was sweet too.

CHAPTER 32
Saturday, October 29th

Courtney called Alex from Ed and Elaine's place, where she sat in her truck in front of their house.

"Hi. Is everything okay?" Worry tinged his question.

"Fine. I'm parked in front of Johnny's parents' house. Johnny isn't home yet, but they called the doctor at the place where he's in recovery. Johnny told them he wanted to talk to me, so I'm headed to Dickinson right now to see him." She adjusted the seat of her truck a little.

"Are you sure you should go there?" The worry had escalated. "He'll be home in a few days."

Courtney hated having him so concerned, but it was time Gary had answers. "Johnny's staying at least another week. They decided it would be better for his recovery to stay longer. Since the police have arrested Doug, they aren't focused on Johnny, so he's able to stay longer."

"Oh…"

The silence weighed on Courtney. "I'll be fine. I'm going for a drive. It's less than an hour away. I'll talk to him and be back before lunch. I'm scheduled to meet with him at 10:00 a.m., and he has something at 10:30. The latest I'll leave Dickinson is 11:00, but probably sooner. I'll text you when I get there and when I'm leaving. How's that?"

"Okay. After talking with Gary and going over everything last night, I'm edgier. This is serious stuff."

"Yes." She hated him worrying this way, but she had to talk with Johnny. "I'll be careful. I promise. I'll stop by the construction site when I'm back. You can see me in person."

"Sounds good. Honor's here at the site, so I'm less concerned about you driving around." His voice changed to a reassuring tone.

Were they pinning too much confidence in Honor's guilt? "You can text me if the situation changes. I should get going now, or Lori and Ed will check on why I'm still parked in their driveway. I love you."

"I love you too. Be careful."

She hung up, suddenly wishing she could forget about the trip and join him at the construction site. She backed up, turned her vehicle, and started for Dickinson, humming along with some cheerful tunes.

Once she reached the clinic and signed all the necessary confidentiality forms, she was ushered into a small sitting room that could comfortably seat around four people. The soft shades of blue on the chairs matched the blue floral fabric on the stuffed armchairs. There were no couches but plenty of elbow room.

When a man walked into the room, she had to look twice before recognizing Johnny. His expression conveyed peace instead of the earlier blank stare. His bleary, red eyes had turned to a soft brown with white rims. He even stood straighter, as if a weight had been lifted. All this despite the death of his brother.

"Hi, Courtney. Thank you for coming to see me." He sat down across from her and leaned against the back of his chair. "I wanted to talk to you sooner, but I wasn't well." A wry smile twisted his lips.

"You look great, Johnny. I'm so sorry about Waylon. That must be hard to deal with along with getting sober." She hadn't realized how hard this conversation would be. She prayed God would help her say the right things.

"Thank you. Not quite the down-and-out bum I appeared before, huh?" He grinned.

"Nope. Pretty spiffy. I bet…" She stopped herself before mentioning Patty.

"The nurse told me you wanted to talk a little more about the day Waylon died."

She interrupted before he could continue, "Only if you want to. I don't want to set your recovery back by bringing up something you'd rather not think about."

He shook his head, his eyes sad. "I'd like to talk about him. No one here knows him, but you've at least met him. Besides, we need to find out what happened to him."

"Do you get any news from anybody about Elm City, or are you completely in the dark about everything that happened after you left?"

"My father asked if I wanted to know what was going on, and I told him no. I think he was afraid I'd leave here before I was well enough to manage 'real life.' Well, that's all we talk about here. Real life. So, from you, I'd like you to tell me." His expression turned serious, and he looked fine to talk about Waylon.

She was glad he would be staying at the rehabilitation center longer. There was a lot of stuff happening. "First of all, yesterday, Doug Bellis was arrested for your brother's murder. We'll have to wait for more information."

"Sure. I understand." Johnny leaned forward in his chair. "But Doug? Why would Doug kill Waylon? I considered maybe Tyson had a brainstorm about Lori or something. Of course, I wasn't thinking clearly a week ago."

She cleared her throat and continued, "Tyson seemed to be trying to help you. He told us he tried to get you to quit drinking when you went out together." Surprised, she watched tears gather in his eyes.

"He was a good friend. He was always saying we wouldn't stay out late when I suggested going out. He'd wait until about beer three, and then he'd always say 'last one.' He knew it wouldn't be, but he tried."

She noticed the past tense and hoped he meant his drinking days with Tyson were over. Or maybe they could have a friendship without the booze.

"I'll have to find something else to do when I get out of here."

"How about fishing? Do you like to fish?" she asked.

"Never tried it." He looked thoughtful. "Might be kind of peaceful out on the water. I don't know if peaceful is Tyson's thing."

"Maybe Lori or your dad?"

He grinned again. "Not Lori. Too many bugs. Probably my dad. Even my mom might be interested. She always used to garden and be outside as much as she could. She deals with depression, and that's been tough lately. Probably where I got my depression genes. I'm worried about how she's dealing with Waylon's death." He shrugged. "I guess I can only do one thing at a time. I need to get well to help her. Anyway, you came to ask about Waylon."

"Right." She wiped the tears from her own eyes. It was miraculous seeing him so with it and outgoing. He'd even trimmed his beard, making it look neater. "Let's start with the jewels."

He groaned. "Yes. The root of all evil in town ever since Honor saw Valerie wearing them. Honor took pictures and showed them around town. Not a smart move. But Valerie realized she'd made a mistake letting everyone see. She was a sharp lady. Poor Gary."

"He's working on his grief and helping with the investigation. Unofficially."

"I figured so. Anyway, here's what Waylon told me the morning he died. We were the first at the construction site because he had some things he wanted to get done before the other guys came in. Valerie hid the jewels the day of the party because she was nervous about someone stealing them. She told Waylon where to find them because she knew our parents and trusted Waylon.

"He couldn't tell me where the jewels were hidden because of my drinking. He decided to tell me the day he died because he had given them to Patty. He planned to quietly give them to Gary or the police the next day. He figured Gary wouldn't arrest Waylon for theft. But then that night

Waylon was murdered. Patty probably didn't know what to do with them.

"I'm not sure how someone found out he'd dug them up. He told me he didn't think anyone saw him, but at least no one was aware Patty had them. I told Waylon he was crazy to involve her. She could get hurt. Someone killed the Millers. They could do the same to Patty."

He appeared angry for the first time since he entered the room. "When I told him to get the jewels to Gary fast and make sure everyone in town knew, so Patty would be safe, he shrugged. Told me it was a secret except for Patty and me."

"Someone realized somehow," Courtney said. "Otherwise, Waylon would still be alive."

"It wasn't me," he said defensively. "I drank too much. Obviously." He swept his hand around the room. "But I'm telling you the truth. I did not tell anyone."

"Not even Tyson when you guys were out drinking?" She had to ask.

"Not even him. Now he's one who can't keep a secret. Has to gloat about anything to do with money or wealth. Otherwise, he's not a bad guy. Lori's safe with him in all the ways that count, even if he and Waylon didn't get along."

"Would he have killed Waylon over anything to do with Lori or for another reason?"

Johnny shook his head before she finished her sentence. "No. He's a little squeamish. I'll keep the story to myself, but he's not someone who could do that."

"Not even in a fit of anger?"

He shook his head again. "Tyson would rather scream out long vocabulary words at you. He can't handle blood or fighting. He's scared of getting hurt. He must have hated Waylon hitting him at the church bake sale and giving him a bloody nose." He paused. "I'm only telling you this to explain why I don't see him killing Waylon, who was twice as big and strong as him."

"Okay. Not Tyson. Back to the jewels. How else would someone know Waylon had them?"

"Was someone else at the construction site when he dug them up?" His voice lifted.

She thought about the holes dug in the backyard at the inn and finding the one behind the shed. Had someone else been poking around after not finding anything in the backyard and saw that hole?

"Who would associate Waylon with the Millers?" she asked. "Who would believe Valerie and Simon would trust him enough to tell him where the jewels were hidden?"

They sat there thinking. Finally, Courtney gave up. "I'll have to think about that part. When you were at our house after you found Waylon, you said he asked you to come over. He had something to tell you. It involved the jewels, but you knew by that time. So, have you come up with something else he might have planned to tell you? Something he'd discovered?"

"I'm thinking he realized who killed the Millers."

At her surprise, he nodded. "Plenty of time between activities around here to think. It's good and bad. I've hurt a lot of people. Maybe if I can figure this out, my parents and Lori will have some respect for me." His sadness returned.

"They love you," she said gently. "I can tell you they wanted to protect you from me today. I had a fine time talking them into checking with the clinic to see if I could visit you. Your sister showed me the fainting goats the first time I visited them at their farm. She misses you."

"Waylon was her favorite," he said matter-of-factly.

"I guess they teach tough love at these places, so I'll just say, so what if he was the favorite? She loves you almost as much as him, or maybe the same amount as him. You can't be sure. Maybe she couldn't show you because you brushed her off? Just saying…"

His eyes lit up, like the idea hit a nerve. "You're right. At first, she and I were closer than Waylon and her."

"Then you got tired of little sister following you around. I have an older brother, by the way. I know what I'm talking about. He's brushed me aside more than once when he wanted guy time and little sister was in the way. I'd say Lori loved you and Waylon equally. Give her a big hug when you get home, if she doesn't beat you to it."

His sweet smile appeared again. She could hardly believe he used to look like a surly grizzly bear and smelled worse.

"Your inn is going to be a hit. And I'm aware of what you want to do one week a month.

Help people who have problems by letting them stay and get psychological and spiritual help. Along with time to think. I used to believe thinking was over-rated."

"Sometimes it is."

"Depends on what you think about."

"Good one," she said. "Since you've been thinking about the Millers and Waylon, do you have any idea who killed them?"

"Two people, definitely. No way to do it by yourself. That narrows it to a few people. It means you need two people who are willing to steal and at least trust each other, for the most part. Not sure they planned to kill the Millers, but either way, they planned to steal those jewels. To move the RV took two people."

"Like who?" she asked, impatient to hear his views.

A young woman popped her head into the room. "Sorry, but I can only give you five more minutes. Group starts soon."

"Thanks, Marsha."

"Thank you for letting me visit," Courtney added.

Marsha nodded and left.

"Okay. Out with it, Johnny. I have to go, and you have to go." She sat forward in the armchair, her elbows on her thighs.

"Right. I don't know, remember. Just guessing." He seemed reluctant to name a name.

"Guessing. No proof," she agreed.

"Right." He took a deep breath, and she almost leapt up and shook him, hoping the names would spill out of his mouth.

"Honor and Doug. Or Doug and Brian. Either Brian or Honor were the brains, and Doug was the hired hand, so to speak. He's too lazy to lay out an elaborate plan. He'd prefer someone set the jewels on the table and walk out of the room, so he could scoop them up. I'm not surprised Doug was arrested for Waylon's death." His brows rose. "Well?"

"We're on the same track. I'll tell you as soon as there's news, or your family will. Doug seems like someone who would rat out anyone else involved if he was part of anything. I'm curious to hear what he's telling the police since he's been arrested." She stood up. "Thanks for talking to me. I'd better go."

He reached out his hand, and she shook it, feeling the warmth of his touch.

"Take care, Johnny. I'm happy for you. I'll call you when we find Waylon's killer, if you're still here, or you'll find out if you're home."

"Thank you. I—"

The nurse stopped at the door.

"We're saying goodbye. One minute, I promise."

She nodded and left.

"When you open your inn, do you think I could maybe use some of the spiritual services being offered?" He dropped his gaze.

She gently touched his arm. Despite his shyness, he was taking steps forward. "Definitely. Free of charge. Deacon Hugh would love to help you."

He smiled at that and met her gaze again. "I better go."

She watched him walk out of the room, marveling at the change God had wrought in him.

CHAPTER 33

About halfway home from visiting Johnny, Courtney noticed someone following her. Being on a one-way highway, at first she thought they were just driving in the same direction, but when she slowed down, they slowed down. When she sped up, so did they. She didn't recognize the vehicle. It had never been parked in the construction area, so probably not Honor. Keeping her eyes on the road and trying to stay ahead of the person, she couldn't get a look at the driver. She didn't see a passenger.

The safest thing to do was call the police and Alex, even if she didn't want to worry him. When he picked up the call, she said, "Now, don't freak out."

"Okay. I'm officially concerned." His sharp tone sounded scared.

"Is Honor there?" Courtney asked.

"She left shortly after you and I talked earlier. Just before you left for Dickinson."

"Okay." Not good. "Did she drive her usual truck?"

"Yes. Why?"

"Someone's following me on the highway, but I don't recognize the vehicle. It's not her usual one, but that doesn't mean she doesn't have access to a different truck we haven't seen."

She had a bad feeling Honor was following her. How she knew to do that, Courtney had no idea. Maybe a sixth sense while watching Alex on the phone with Courtney earlier? He probably exuded anxiety, which Honor picked up on. She'd probably kept her guard up ever since the police arrested Doug.

"Call Gary and tell him I'm being followed." She gave him the mile marker she'd just passed. "Maybe they can get the Highway Patrol to pull her over—stop her long enough for me to get home. Don't forget the tracker on my phone if we lose connection."

"Stay on the line. I'm borrowing someone else's phone to call Gary."

"Hey, Robb," he shouted in the background. "Can I borrow your phone?"

Robb must have joined Alex, because she heard him say, "Sure. What's going on?"

"I'm worried about Courtney. Let's go outside," Alex said.

The vehicle crept closer. "Hurry, Alex," she whispered. *God, please send help.*

She decided to speed instead of slow down. She stepped on the gas. Maybe the police would pull her over. She didn't care at this point.

She was vaguely aware of the discussion between Robb, Alex, and the police.

"Courtney?" Alex's voice came clearly again.

"I'm still here. I decided to speed up. Maybe I'll be the one who gets stopped."

"I understand what you're doing, but maybe you should slow down." His voice rose toward the end.

She knew he wanted to say, if an accident occurred, she'd have a better chance of living if they were going at a slower speed.

"Hang in there. They told us one of the highway patrol officers isn't far from where you are. They should be there within a few minutes."

"Good, because the car behind me has sped up." She didn't like the swirling in her stomach. Would the person ram her truck from behind? Push her off the road? She slowed down suddenly and breathed a sigh of relief when she saw the patrol car parked on the shoulder of the highway.

She put on speed and passed. So did the person following. They must have been told to let Courtney go, because the patrolman let her pass and then put on the lights and siren as he pulled up beside the vehicle behind her.

The truck put on a burst of speed and passed Courtney, almost sideswiping her when it zoomed into the passing lane. The patrolman chasing after it had to drop back for a moment to avoid a crash. Once the person passed Courtney, the police car sped up, and they soon left Courtney behind as they pulled ahead.

She still couldn't get a look at the driver. She'd been too busy keeping her own vehicle on the road. Finally, as they came over a hill, another patrol car sat on the side of the road.

At this point, Courtney was going the speed limit and slowed even more while moving to the right lane, so the patrolman on the side of the road could join the chase ahead of her. The second patrol car followed the first, and the person who was behind Courtney finally pulled off to the side of the highway.

Courtney breathed a sigh of relief. She'd finally find out who caused some of the bad things happening in Elm City.

She fully expected Honor to be in the truck on the shoulder between the two patrol cars. When Courtney passed them, she slowed down, thanking God no other traffic was around at the moment. She parked on the shoulder of the road, far enough ahead of the unfolding scene behind her but close enough to have some idea of what happened.

She was a little concerned because the brief glimpse of the woman behind the wheel of the truck when she passed didn't look like Honor. This woman had dark hair, not blonde like Honor.

The woman got out of the vehicle and ran. The patrolmen chased her down into the ditch, tackled her, frisked and handcuffed her. What did the woman think she'd accomplish? There was nowhere to go.

She heard another siren, and a police car drove past her and parked in front of her. She watched the front door open. Gary stepped out of the car.

She breathed a sigh of relief and returned to her phone call. Alex had stayed on the line. "Hey, Alex. Sorry. I was busy watching the road, and the police stopped and handcuffed whoever is behind me. She ran, but I didn't get a good look. Her hair was dark. Gary's arrived." She heard a gusty sigh of relief on the other end of the line. "I'm parked ahead of the patrolmen, waiting for them to get to me. They've just put the woman in the back of one of the patrol cars."

"Well, I'm thankful they're on the scene, and she's been taken into custody. Gary can run interference if necessary. I bet he can't wait to find out who they've arrested. He should be able to help you stay out of trouble." His shaky laugh tore through her.

Her legs shook as adrenaline hit. "We can talk about my visit with Johnny to take up some time." She glanced in her rearview mirror. "Or not. The police are headed this way."

Both highway patrolmen's vehicles pulled up, one in front of her and one behind her. The mystery person's vehicle sat empty on the side of the road.

Courtney hit the button to roll down the window and held her hands at the top of the steering wheel with her phone still in one hand. "They've parked in front of and behind me. I'm waiting for them to approach. I wonder what the other driver told them."

"Don't worry. Your story will match what Gary and I told them. They only have to call the sheriff to confirm what's going on," Alex reassured her. A few minutes of restless waiting passed.

"Gary's stopped them and is talking to them. Right. Here they come. You okay?" she asked him.

"Yes. Now that Gary's there." He did sound more relaxed.

.   "I'll be fine. I'll check in with you when I'm heading home."

"Okay. I love you."

She knew he didn't want to hang up. "I love you too." After ending the call, she put her phone in her jacket pocket.

"Hello, ma'am. Can you please step out of the vehicle, keeping your hands where we can see them?" One of the patrolmen stood a few feet away. He reached over, opened her door and stepped back a few paces. The other patrolman stood to the side and back of him.

Gary shrugged and nodded.

She stepped out of the vehicle, holding up her hands about shoulder high.

"What's your name?" The young officer in front of her reminded her a little of Tyson with his dark hair, although Tyson didn't usually wear a grim expression and sunglasses.

"Courtney Richmond." She wondered if they'd left the woman in the police vehicle by herself, or if there was another officer with her.

"Okay." He nodded to the other officer, who left them and walked back to the other patrol car. "You can put down your hands now," he said. "Do you have identification? Deputy Lachlan says he knows you, but this sounds like a big case, and we're doing everything by the book."

Her hands shook, and she took a deep breath. "Do you mind if I lean against my vehicle for a minute? I'm suddenly faint." She rested against the back of the truck and fought the dizziness. No, she didn't want to throw up.

The officer's attention never wavered.

She slowly stood straight. "I'm okay now. Sorry about that. My identification is in my purse. Can I get it off the seat?"

"Yes."

Gary stood back while the patrolman watched closely as she grabbed her purse and rummaged in it. She handed over her driver's license.

After a quick glance between her and the license, he nodded at Gary. "I'll give this to Patrolman Watson and be back soon." He went over to the other car and handed her driver's license in through the window. He stood there waiting.

Gary glanced down at her. "Are you all right?"

"Just fine." She paced a few steps. "I want to get back there and see who that woman is. Don't you?"

His laugh captured the attention of the patrolman waiting for Courtney's license to be run through the system.

"Definitely. But if this is one of my parents' killers, the patrolman is right. We need to follow the law and make sure, when the case comes to court, the guilty person doesn't have a way to get out of the murder charge." He grimaced.

The patrolman rejoined them, handing Courtney her license. She stuck it in her pocket with her phone. Everything must have checked out, because he didn't say anything about her license.

"I'm Patrolman Neeson," he told Gary.

Gary held out his hand. "Deputy Lachlan. A friend of Courtney's."

They shook hands, and Patrolman Neeson turned to Courtney. "We got a report you thought that woman was following you." He nodded toward the other patrol car.

"I thought so. I didn't get a good look at her, so I'm not sure if I know her." She shivered.

"How about taking a look now?" he asked.

"You want me to go see her?" Courtney's queasiness returned even though she was getting exactly what she wanted. "Sure. If it has anything to do with what's going in Elm City, I definitely want to see who it is." She walked beside the officer, feeling stronger with each step. Were they going finally getting their answer?

Gary followed behind.

"What's this have to do with Elm City?" Patrolman Neeson asked.

"Have you ever heard of the Millers who disappeared eight years ago?" Courtney asked him. "Their RV was gone the morning they were supposed to move to Virginia, so no one thought anything of it. Then the people in Virginia, who expected the Millers to take possession of their house, called and said they didn't show up." Talking helped her keep her mind calm before the coming confrontation.

"All the older guys in the department talk about it. I was too young to hear about the disappearance until I started working. We all want to be the one to solve it," he said.

"Well, you might get to arrest one of the people involved. But you might want to tone down the enthusiasm since it involves Gary's parents' death." She glanced back at Gary, who focused his gaze on the ground.

"Really?" The patrolman stopped and looked at her.

She looked back at Gary.

He nodded his agreement.

"If I'm right, this woman is part of it." It looked like that made his day, as a small smile appeared—but disappeared quickly. "By the way, Gary wants to see who might have killed his parents."

The patrolman stopped. "I don't know if we can allow him to talk to her."

His hesitation didn't stop Courtney or Gary. They continued walking the final ten feet to the car holding the long-awaited answer.

Courtney paused a few feet from the car. "He deserves to be here. We'll keep him away from her as much as possible."

Patrolman Watson got out of the vehicle and addressed Patrolman Neeson, "Everything checks out."

Neeson nodded and looked at Gary. "This is Deputy Gary Lachlan, and the situation might involve his parents. We decided, after eight years, he deserves to be here, but he'll keep out of it as much as possible."

Patrolman Watson, more seasoned than his fellow patrolman, looked Gary over. "Great. Wait a minute before opening the door though."

Both the patrol officers stood in front of the back door, and Gary was trying to get a view inside the car. So was Courtney, but a little less obviously. "We might have a killer, so be on your guard. The case from Elm City."

"The stabbing?" the older cop asked.

"Right. And a couple who disappeared eight years ago."

"The Millers." The older patrol officer stared at Courtney. "If that's who we have, you've solved a case we've all wanted to close."

"Thanks. But Gary helped." She pointed at him. "The Millers are his parents."

Finally, he nodded his approval.

They reached the back door of the car, where the other older officer stood waiting. Then he nodded at the younger patrolman.

"Oh." The older guy reached out and shook Gary's hand. "Sorry, man. Didn't know."

"No problem, but I'm losing patience." Gary moved back and forth in front of the patrolmen. "Can we see her?"

Patrolman Neeson said, "Stand behind me. She's cuffed, but we're not taking chances." He nodded to the other patrolman, who opened the door.

She and Gary stepped around him quickly. Her palms turned damp, her heart racing as she took another step forward and peered into the back seat of the patrol car. Gary's breath shivered down her neck.

CHAPTER 34

Courtney's world made one quick revolution before the dizziness passed. "Janine! What were you doing?"

Tears streamed down her face. She kicked the seat in front of her. "What did it look like I was doing, you ninny?! Trying to get rid of you. You've ruined everything!" She screamed and kicked the seat again before glancing over Courtney's shoulder. "Let me out of here!" she yelled at Gary.

"Right. That's exactly what I'm going to do," Gary grunted, "when we get to the police station. I hear there's a cell with your name on it."

Courtney's mind churned, finally settling on the fact Janine tried to kill her, not Honor. "You tried to kill me by running me off the road." She finally understood what happened to the Millers. "And you and Honor didn't go to Bismarck for a spa day. You went with Honor or Brian to the

Millers' to steal the jewels—and you killed them. Why did you kill them?"

"So she is our killer?" one of the patrolmen asked.

Courtney had her back to them, so she wasn't sure which one spoke. "Yes. The Millers from Elm City eight years ago, and Waylon Frederickson a few days ago. Check with Sheriff Warren."

An officer warned, "Maybe you want to back away from her."

She glanced at them. "She's cuffed, and you're right there. And Gary's right here too. I don't think she wants to fight it out with Gary. She can't get far. I have questions about what she did."

Gary's face was set like granite, his jaws moving. "Why did you kill my parents?"

"You're a guy. You wouldn't understand." Defeat etched every line of her face.

Maybe they were just as curious to hear Janine's answers as Courtney, because the patrolmen didn't interfere. She took that as permission to continue asking questions with Gary. She looked back at Janine. "Why?"

Janine turned toward her, tears streaming down her face. "I don't think you'd understand the reason either. Has Alex ever hit you?"

Courtney took a step back in surprise and bumped into Gary. "No, of course not. Did Brian hit you? Was that the reason you wanted the jewels?"

Something felt wrong, but Courtney couldn't pinpoint her unease. Instead of the fear she'd expected to see in Janine's eyes, she caught a glimpse of calculation. Or was that her imagination? Was Janine lying to them?

"Brian likes to be the man of the house. Ordering me around and hitting me once in a while. I thought I could sell the jewels and have enough money to leave him, but it didn't work out. Then I got pregnant.

"Honor just wants her construction company." She sniffed. "As if that'll make her happy. I have the children to think of now. Brian would take them away from me, and I don't know what he'd do to them. I grew up poor. I didn't want to run away with no money like Mom did."

"There are places to help women who are abused." Gary's tone was flat.

How did he really feel? She turned around to look at him. His hands were clenched into fists. "Your husbands did go fishing or lazed around all day recovering from their hangovers. And Doug didn't kill Waylon. You or Honor did."

Janine smirked before dissolving into tears again. "Like Honor could pull it off without me. It really helps to play the helpless female role. You thought Honor was the brains behind everything. She didn't want to kill them. I told her they'd be chasing us all our lives if we let them live."

Courtney shivered at the way Janine described that night eight years ago. She sounded proud of what she'd done. And her quick change from smiling to tears. Like an act.

Janine shook her head in disgust. "Honor only thinks she's smart. She's lucky she lives with a lazy guy. If she'd married someone like Brian, she'd have learned life can get really hard. She thinks she has it bad."

"So, this was all because you wanted to escape Brian?" Courtney tried to wrap her mind around killing someone to escape someone else. "Why didn't you leave or kill him?"

"Who's the first suspect if a married guy is murdered?" She didn't wait for an answer. "The wife. I needed to get the funds together to hide successfully. If you'd ever been in an abusive relationship, you'd understand they never let you go. They stalk you until you're too worn out to care about anything. And those women's shelters don't do enough. I've seen what can happen." Janine desperately gazed around the back seat of the patrol car.

"Except you killed innocent people."

Gary's staccato statement made Courtney jump.

Janine rolled her eyes and turned away, looking out the opposite window. "Like I said, you don't understand. Probably never will."

"Well, I might not, but killing people isn't the answer either. Now you'll be getting away from Brian for good." Courtney didn't feel right having said that part, but it just slipped out.

She stepped back, along with Gary.

"Who helped you?" he asked.

"Who do you think? Honor. She thought she'd convinced me, but I was the boss." She tossed her head so her hair slid over her shoulder.

Gary stared at her. "Since you're throwing Brian to the wolves about abuse, you would have been better off lying and saying Brian forced you."

A calculating look in her eyes disappeared, and her face crumpled. As she screamed obscenities, Gary slammed the door closed.

Courtney turned to the patrolman. "Sorry for the rant. Her name is Janine Lang. Honor Bellis was her partner in the murders, according to what she's said. I'm guessing Janine killed Waylon without Honor's help, but I could be wrong.

"I'm done with her." Gary turned his back on the patrol car and Janine. "I'm sure you'll get all the help you need from Sheriff Warren. I'll wait in my vehicle for you to question me."

Courtney stomped back to her own truck, angry at the devastation Janine caused. Gary didn't seem to want to talk right now, but she and Alex would be available when he was ready. A semi passed them on the highway, almost blowing her off the road. After it passed them, she heard the patrolmen talking but too quietly to hear their words.

Janine calmed down with the lack of an audience. Patrolmen Watson said to his partner, "I'll take her in. We'll start charges with fleeing from the police and speeding. The county will add more charges."

"I think they will too," Courtney called to them from where she leaned against her back bumper before the other patrolman could say anything. She stood there for a minute, shaking her head.

Patrolman Watson drove off with Janine, and Patrolman Neeson joined her and Gary on the side of the road. Gary said, "Come on. Time to get you back home."

"Oh, right. Sorry, I can't believe it's her. I expected someone else. I would never have suspected Janine," she repeated.

Gary and the patrolman followed her to her truck's driver's side. "I hope you weren't on that phone while you were driving," he said.

"Nope. I used my speaker and changed to holding the phone when I pulled to the side of the road."

"Just checking."

She noticed a slight upturn at the corner of his mouth.

"How did you know about Deputy Lachlan's parents? Or do you live in Elm City?" he asked.

She smiled at Gary. "My husband and I bought the Millers' house from Gary to renovate it into an inn."

He took off his sunglasses and held out his hand. Surprised, she shook it.

"Congratulations on helping solve the case." He reached over to Gary. "I'm sorry about your parents. I've been following the case all these years, wondering what happened. And when they found the bones…it was fascinating." He flushed. "Sorry. Bad taste."

"Don't worry." Gary summoned up a weary smile. "I'm used to the interest."

"I can give you an escort home if Gary can't make it," the patrolman told Courtney.

"Thank you. Did I say thanks for rescuing me? Thank you for that too."

He gave her a full smile. "Doing my duty. And we're not far from Elm City, so it's not a problem to escort you. In fact, if Deputy Lachlan can't follow you, you'd be safer to have someone else around. I've heard the Millers were killed by at least two people, and the other one hasn't been apprehended yet. You mentioned Honor Bellis. Right?"

"Right." She thought about Honor being gone from the construction site and wondered where she was. "I appreciate it. I thought I was going to die today." She pulled out her phone to call Alex as soon as she had an escort home.

"Gary, the patrolman can follow me. We're only about twenty minutes from Elm City, so if you want to head back, you can."

"I'll escort you. No need to bother Patrolman Neeson further." He looked at him. "Thanks for saving Courtney. My husband and I are very grateful."

"You're welcome." His face reddened under the tan.

She opened her vehicle door, and the patrolman waited until she'd closed it. The window was still down. "Do you want a statement from me?"

"A short one. I have a lot from what you said to Mrs. Lang." He put on his sunglasses and pulled out a notebook. "We're also being recorded by my body camera."

"Maybe she didn't care if she lived or not if Brian was abusing her. Sorry, that's speculation. Anyway, I thought it was Honor Bellis driving— the woman I think Janine joined forces with to steal jewelry from the Millers and kill them. That also is a guess, so I'll leave it to you and other law enforcement to prove or disprove my theory. That covers everything I can think of."

She was suddenly tired and wanted to get home to Alex.

"Whose vehicle was Janine driving?" Gary asked.

The patrolman flipped a few pages in his notebook. "The vehicle is registered to a Beatrice Crow. When we called, she didn't know it was missing. I understand she rarely drives."

"She's in her eighties," Gary said. "I'm not surprised she didn't notice."

"That explains why I didn't recognize it," Courtney said. "I'm ready to go home."

"Okay. You might have to come to one of the stations, depending on jurisdiction, and sign a statement tomorrow. Obviously, this is part of an ongoing investigation, so it will probably be someone else contacting you.”

“That’s fine. I’ll be happy to help.” And she would. Finally, most of the pieces had fallen into place.

He stuffed his notebook back into his pocket. “You have a good day. Both of you.” He lifted his hand in a half wave and strode back to his car.

“Okay. I’ll wait until you’ve pulled out in your vehicle, then I’ll follow,” Gary said.

“Great. It’ll give me a chance to reassure Alex with a quick call first.”

He smiled his understanding.

Courtney called Alex, talking hands-free all the way to Elm City with Gary following her. She filled Alex in on all the details.

Gary honked once when she pulled into her driveway and pulled over to the curb.

She walked over to him. “Thanks for the escort.”

“I see you have a welcoming committee.” Gary gazed at the house.

She looked at the front of the house where Alex stood on the top step waiting.

"Come for food and to talk at six," Courtney suggested to Gary.

"Thanks for the invitation. I'll be there at six unless they let me listen to interviews. I'll let you know." He waved at Alex, said goodbye to Courtney, and drove away.

Courtney ran up the steps, and Alex pulled her into a tight hug before kissing her senseless.

CHAPTER 35

As the afternoon moved forward, Courtney continued thinking more about Janine's demeanor, and something was wrong. She knew Janine lied about something. She considered whether Brian had abused Janine and decided to visit him. If he was an abuser, she wasn't going alone.

She stood in the kitchen doorway of their house and looked at Alex working on paperwork at the table. "Hey there."

He glanced at her. "How are you doing?"

"Oh, I'm fine." After a quiet lunch with Alex and a brief nap, her sweaty palms disappeared. "Would you like to go with me to see Brian? Something's wrong with Janine's story, and I want to talk to him. You don't want me to go alone."

He pushed his chair back and stood to join her. "I'll come. I won't be letting you out of my sight for a few days. I never want to be that scared again. My concentration was patchy anyway."

Alex drove while Courtney ran a few questions through her mind, wondering about the best approach. The farmhouse and grounds were as well maintained as they'd been when she visited a few weeks ago to give the couple their paychecks. But the place reminded her of a ghost town. Quiet. The children were obviously in school.

The front door opened, and Brian stepped outside. He came down the steps to greet them, shoulders drooping. There was no flirting or muscle display today.

"I'm so sorry." He stood as if waiting for a punch from one of them. "I didn't know about Janine and Honor, although I should have guessed."

"We're not here to blame you." Courtney actually felt sorry for him. This didn't look like an abuser. Maybe he wasn't. Janine had told them he was, but how reliable was her word? However, abusers sometimes hid in plain sight, so he could be one. "Do you want to sit down at the picnic table?"

Brian nodded, and Alex waited until he was seated before joining him on his side of the picnic table.

Courtney sat across from them. How had she become the hostess at Brian's place? "Janine's claiming you've abused her for years, and she wanted the money from the jewelry to flee."

He dropped his head. "She told me if I ever told the truth, she'd claim I was abusing her."

"The truth about what?" Courtney noted the word "claim."

"She's the one abusing me." His bitter laugh disturbed the quiet, sending chills down Courtney's back. He looked up and held eye contact. "I didn't want to leave my family farm to her, and she wouldn't go away, even when I offered to pay her expenses. I finally got up the courage to leave after the Millers disappeared."

"You knew she had something to do with their disappearance?" Courtney couldn't believe he'd keep quiet, even if Janine abused him.

"No! No way would I have let someone suffer for years if I'd known. Gary's a great guy." He glanced at Alex. "I would have told him years ago. It never occurred to me Janine had anything to do with what happened to his parents. I bought the story that she and Honor went to Bismarck for the day. Her leaving me to do the chores was her way of punishing me for letting loose with the fireworks the night before. At least I thought that for years. It was her usual way of getting back at me for any imagined things I'd done wrong."

He shook his head and looked into the distance. "Like I said, I was ready to leave, and then she told me she was pregnant. I couldn't leave after that. I always wondered why she chose me. I guess because the farm was doing well, and I was taken in by her meek, 'poor me' act. I found out I'd made a mistake after our honeymoon, when we had our first fight. It involved a knife, and I wasn't the one holding it."

He stood up and stepped back from the picnic table. "You don't believe me."

Alex leapt off the bench, his eyes pinned on Brian.

As he noted Alex's wary look, the bitter laugh sounded again. "No need to worry. I'm just going to show you something, and we can sit down again." Brian pulled off his t-shirt and slowly turned around in a circle.

Courtney gasped at the crisscrossed wounds. Most were healed, but there were a few newer ones.

He put his shirt back on and sat down. "She likes to use the knife when I fall asleep. I grabbed her wrists too tightly one time to stop her. She showed Honor and told her I was hurting her. Honor believed her. Now Janine uses it as a warning whenever I try and stop her. She's the one abusing me, not the other way around."

"Why don't you leave?" Courtney couldn't understand a strong man like Brian reduced to this defeated victim. "Why don't you show someone, a doctor or the police, what you've shown us? I believe you."

"I do too." Alex placed a hand on Brian's hands, which were clenched together on top of the table. "We can help."

Brian took a deep breath. "I can't have my children taken away from me. They're the only reason I stayed. She would have ruined them if I'd left them with her. She would have also accused me of being the abuser if I'd taken them away. I don't think she loves them. She uses them for the power." He started crying.

Courtney wondered how Brian withstood the pressure all these years with no one to believe him, no one to help him, and everything that appeared like an answer had a huge downside. Janine held all the power, and he was right. She was accusing him of abuse.

They sat with him while he cried. Courtney silently prayed for God to give Brian peace and to show her and Alex how to help him. Everything was going to come out now.

Brian's tears came to an end, and he sniffled a few times. "Sorry." He gazed around the farm, anywhere but at them. "The police called before you came. They told me social services would pick the children up from school. They told me to stay away, but I have to be there and reassure the kids to go with them."

"We'll do whatever we can." Alex stood and placed his hand on Brian's shoulder.

Courtney noticed him flinch. Brian hadn't been playing a part. "Do you have something you need us to do for you?"

He finally made eye contact, his eyes red. "No, thank you. I'm fine."

"You don't have to be alone any longer. Courtney and I will give you a ride to the school. We'll talk to the police for you. We're friends with Gary. He trusts us. We'll put in a good word."

Alex added gently, "They're going to come talk to you at some point."

Brian nodded. "I figured."

"Show them what you showed us. If they decide to detain you, give us a call. We'll get you an attorney. I know a good one." Courtney stood. She already planned to let Gary in on how Janine played them all. She'd also contact her brother Nathan, an attorney. "We'll leave you for now, but don't hesitate to contact us. We mean it, Brian. We'll be back in an hour to be with you when Child Protection Services arrives. If the police come before that, send us a text."

"Thank you." He sat there, his eyes sad, and watched them drive away.

Courtney touched Alex's arm while he drove. "That's a bad deal. I'm so glad we came out here. I'm going to contact Gary. I hope he can answer his phone right now."

She pulled her cell phone out of her pocket and called him. "Hi. I didn't know if you would answer."

"Janine's called for an attorney, so we're waiting for them to arrive. You wouldn't call if it weren't important." He sounded tired.

"We just left Brian. He's given us some information we think the police will want to check out. He said he's the one who's being abused, not Janine." She waited for a response.

"You're kidding." He didn't sound like he bought the idea.

"Think about it. Isn't Janine unstable? Doesn't she seem remorseless over what she did to your parents? You should see Brian's back and stomach. He's got a bunch of knife wounds all over. Some older. Some new. I really think this needs to be considered." She waited.

"That's a twist I didn't see." His words came slowly, as if he was really considering the news about Brian.

"Can you get word to the social service department before CPS interviews the children? Maybe Mom treats them mean, but Dad doesn't? I don't know how it works." Courtney didn't want to jump to conclusions. Brian could be the liar and not Janine, but Brian gave more proof than Janine. And she already lied.

"That's a good idea. I'll plant some seeds around here about the children. They can check if Janine has ever had medical care or anything documented indicating abuse by Brian."

"I believed Brian today, but who knows? I'll let you get back to business and figure out who's telling the truth."

"Thanks for the heads-up, Courtney. I'll have them check it all out. Bye."

After she put her phone back in her pocket, she glanced at Alex. "What do you think?"

"Something happened to Brian. The police will look for evidence."

"Can't wait to hear more from Gary." Her sympathy rested with Brian. Was he a great actor? Or was it real? "How this will go down with the police? Who are they going to believe? Janine or Brian?"

***

Alex and Courtney arrived at Brian's farm again. His truck was in the yard, and the kids were playing outside as school had finished for the day.

Brian came out of the house and was greeted with a hug from the youngest child. The other two hung back a little, staring at Alex and Courtney. They grinned at their dad, though.

As Alex and Courtney approached Brian, the older children joined them and stood by Brian. There were two girls and a boy. They appeared to be ages five to eight.

"I have something to tell you." Brian was interrupted by the sound of a vehicle, and they all turned to find a car approaching. The woman behind the wheel appeared to be in her thirties and parked beside Alex's truck in the driveway. She approached the group and smiled at the group.

She reached out her hand to Brian. "I'm Marjorie Henson. You can all call me Marj." She smiled kindly at the children before turning to Alex and Courtney. She held out her hand to them. "Hello."

Alex introduced himself and Courtney as they shook Marj's hand. "We're here for support."

"Great. Glad to have you here." The smile didn't leave her face. She turned to look at the children again. "Has your dad told you about me yet?"

They all shook their heads and moved closer to Brian, gazing up at him in question.

Brian crouched down in front of the children. "This lady is going to watch you for a little while. She'll talk to you, and then she'll bring you home again. Kind of like a babysitter."

The youngest girl started crying and clinging to his shirt. "I don't want to go with her, Daddy. I want to stay with you."

Brian pulled her into a hug and stroked her hair. "I know, honey, but it won't be for very long. You'll be okay. And you'll be with your brother and sister." He held her away a little and looked into her tearstained face.

Courtney almost started crying at the tenderness in his gaze. He was making promises he might not be able to keep. Brian's face appeared serene, but she caught a hint of anguish in his eyes, which he hid from his children.

"It is for a few hours only, right?" Brian asked Marj.

"Right." She crouched down to the level of the children. "As your dad said, you'll only be with me for a short time, and then I'll bring you right back. Okay?"

"Promise?" The boy asked, tears pooling in his eyes too. He refused to let them fall.

"Promise." She grinned at him. "We'll try and have fun, okay?"

"Okay." He nodded, after looking up at his dad, who gave him a smile back.

Brian said cheerfully, "You go with her and answer her questions, and then you can come home." He stood and patted her on the head then looked at his other two children. Stress tinged his voice. "You two okay?"

"Yes." Twin expressions of uneasiness showed they weren't.

"Like I said, answer her questions, and this will all be over soon." He hugged them all to him.

"The truth?" the boy asked.

Brian's face softened further. "The real truth, the whole truth."

"May I speak to you for a moment, Mr. Lang?" Marj stepped away a few feet, out of earshot, and waited for Brian to follow.

Courtney stepped over to stand by Brian, and Alex stayed with the children. He got down on his haunches like Brian. "Hi. I'm Alex. I'm your dad's friend." He smiled at them.

"Oh, Dad talked about you. You're his boss," the little boy said.

"Exactly. You can call me Alex like he does. What are your names?"

Courtney missed the rest of the conversation as she tuned into Marjorie's question.

She looked concerned as she turned her face away from the children. "Was that code for something?"

He looked puzzled. "What?"

"When you said, 'The real truth, the whole truth.' Did that mean something special?" She eyed him the way a police officer would, skepticism oozing out of every pore.

"No. It means what it means. Tell you the truth, no matter who gets in trouble." Brian held her gaze. "Including me. Children aren't to be used to settle adult matters. I want the best for them."

"Okay." Her face softened. "I'll take good care of them." She walked back over to the kids, gathered them together, and left.

The youngest had stared longingly back at her father. The other two stoically did what they were told, although they dragged their feet as if they'd done many things they didn't want to do in their young lives.

"I hope Gary gets to the truth soon." Brian's grim expression led to a moment of quiet. "Thank you for your help and support." He shook hands and waited for them to get in their truck.

"If you need help, call us." Alex patted him on the back before he got into the driver's seat.

Brian nod and turned and walked slowly to his quiet house.

"I agree with his wish. I hope the truth comes out soon." Courtney shifted in her seat. "Whichever one of those two is abusing the other, those children need to be with someone who loves them and treats them well."

CHAPTER 36

Gary called at 4:00 p.m., and Courtney wondered what he had to say that couldn't wait until dinner.

"I can't make it this evening." A note of elation carried across the air to her. "They're letting me see the interviews from behind the glass. I never thought I'd be here for this moment."

"That's great, Gary. I'm jealous, although I got my fill of Janine this morning. I'm so happy they're letting you hear what's going on."

"Sheriff Warren told them what we've been doing to solve the case, and they agreed, as long as I don't speak to anyone outside law enforcement, I can stay and watch the interviews."

"I'm so happy for you. You'll let us know if there's anything new, won't you?" she asked.

"Definitely. So far they've charged Janine. She confessed she shot my parents. Honor's being held for questioning, and they still haven't let Doug go. I owe you and Alex a lot for bringing this long search to a close. I hope to hear they have enough evidence for trials. I better go. They just brought in Doug to see what he has to say.”

“Thanks for calling. Talk to you soon.” She was envious she couldn’t join Gary and hear what the interviewees said.

Alex hovered around Courtney for the evening. She didn’t mind, except she was sorry he’d been so worried.

“Did Honor ever return to the construction site?” Courtney couldn’t believe she forgot about her.

“Yes, she did. Right after you called and said you were being followed. She was arrested around 2:00 p.m. I should have told you, but in the heat of the moment, I wasn’t thinking clearly. I was afraid for you.”

They were back on the couch with the television on low volume. She wondered if the sofa would last another week if they kept spending so much time sitting on it talking about the cases.

“Any idea what Honor did while she was gone from the site?” Courtney tucked her feet under her.

Alex smiled—a devious smile she'd only seen a few times.

"What did you do?" She grabbed his arm.

"I had her followed." He kept grinning.

"You what!?" she sputtered. He'd totally surprised her.

"Well, you scared me, searching for a killer or two, and since we were pretty sure Honor was the leader of all the bad stuff, I thought, why not?" His face changed as he spoke, and by the time he finished, his mouth set in a grim line. "I was worried."

She leaned back, unable to respond for a minute. "I'm sorry." The fatigue and fear of the day caught up with her, and she started sobbing.

He pulled her close and held her. "My having Honor followed made you cry?" Puzzlement sounded in his voice.

She shook her head. She couldn't speak yet. Finally, she stopped crying and went to get a few tissues. After sitting beside him again, she took his hand and twirled his wedding ring. "For better or worse. Wow. You bring new meaning to the words for worse."

"So you're not mad at me?" He put his hand over hers.

"No." She held back more tears. "I'm touched. That you love me that much." She offered him a soft smile. "You surprised me, and it hit me I've really been thinking of what I want so long, I didn't even ask you what you want."

"For you to be happy," he replied so quickly, she knew it was the truth. "I want to let you follow your heart."

"Investigating murder?" What husband was okay with that? Well, not okay with it so much as accepting her actions, even when she worried him. "Thank you."

She hugged him and leaned back against the couch, spent. "Who followed Honor, and what did they find out?"

"Izzy."

"What?" Her surprise made him laugh.

"She wanted to help, and we kind of trust her, and she was free, so… Anyway, Honor went to see an attorney," he said.

"Oh. Probably hiring someone for Doug."

He shook his head. "No. This attorney specializes in divorces."

Another surprise. "She's not wasting any time in moving away from Doug. Does she think she can get out of the Millers' murder somehow?"

"How could she do that? Janine's making it clear Honor went along every step of the way," Alex pointed out.

She thought about that. "I don't know. But I really want more details about Waylon's death before I tell Johnny."

"Good idea, but I doubt we're going to get answers tonight," Alex said. "I want to enjoy the rest of the evening with you by my side and no more talk of murder or jewels." His tone was firm.

"Agreed." She leaned against him, and he put his arm around her as they watched television. Or pretended to. Her mind was still on the murders until she fell asleep.

CHAPTER 37
Sunday, October 30th

Courtney woke up the next morning, looking around the room. She'd fallen asleep on the couch, and Alex gave her a pillow and blanket without her waking up. She smiled. He was one of a kind.

Hiring an investigator to follow Honor and not telling her—well, at least he was a team player. She needed to do something for him in return. Not because he expected it, but because she loved him, and he deserved some attention from her that had nothing to do with the inn or murder investigations.

While she ate breakfast, she pondered the jewelry situation and how they could prove eight years later that Honor and Janine killed the Millers. A niggling started when she remembered what Gary said about his mother wearing all sorts of rings, some inexpensive, some not.

What would Valerie have done with the inexpensive ones? She wouldn't have hidden them with the other jewels. She would have kept them in a jewelry box. And a lot of women also had everyday earrings.

She left half her coffee in the cup and ran for her cell phone. She dialed the number for Izzy Collins, relieved when she answered. After the usual greetings, she asked her question.

"Izzy, did Valerie own earrings and rings or other jewelry she wore on a regular basis? Not precious gemstones or metals, but everyday costume jewelry, something she might have been wearing the night of the Fourth of July party?"

"Oh, sure. She always wore a watch. We laughed at her because everyone else checked the time on their phones. Watches are out of style. She laughed too and said she didn't care. It was a fashion watch." Izzy fell silent.

"Was it expensive?" Courtney's excitement built.

"I'm not sure. It might have been gold, but it might have been gold-plated. Simon gave it to her for their tenth anniversary. It had an inscription on the back. An inside joke for them." She laughed.

"They shared the story, so it wasn't exactly a secret."

"What did it say?"

"Happy tenth anniversary. Hope to add another zero someday." Izzy's voice trailed off, and she sniffed. "They didn't get that extra zero."

Courtney was confused. *Another zero?* "What did that mean, another zero? Sounds like not getting something rather than adding something?"

"Simon was referencing the number ten for their tenth anniversary. Add a zero to the ten, and you get one hundred. One hundred years together."

"Oh." Sad and sweet.

"Is there anything else?" Izzy asked.

Courtney realized she'd been silent too long, considering Izzy's story. "How about earrings? If someone pierces their ears, they sometimes leave earrings in all the time."

"Interesting you should say that. I totally forgot. She had emerald-cut diamond earrings she wore most of the time. Now, those were expensive. They were a good size but not too big." Izzy's voice faded for a minute, then returned full force, "I might have a picture of Valerie wearing those earrings."

Courtney's heart started racing. "Really?"

"We took pictures the night of the party. Valerie and Simon, then myself, Finn, and Valerie and Simon. Some of Brian, Janine, Honor, and Doug."

Courtney heard rustling on the other end of the phone.

"I'm wondering if I uploaded those to the cloud or not. Just a minute."

Oh, God, she prayed. *Please let Izzy find a copy of the pictures.*

"Ah," Izzy came back on the line, "it looks like I have pictures from eight years ago, but I'll have to search through a bunch of them to find the ones I want."

"I hate to ask, but I'm going to anyway." Courtney wanted to shout her excitement. "Can you check now? They might help the police."

"Definitely. I'll go through them right away. I want Valerie and Simon to finally have justice. I'll hopefully call you back soon."

"Thanks so much, Izzy." She hung up, praying again.

She called Alex and told him what she'd done. "I'm praying as hard as I can Izzy finds those pictures, and the police can search for those items."

"I'll add my prayers," Alex assured her. "Did you sleep well?"

"Definitely. Thanks for the blanket and pillow. That was thoughtful of you."

"You were snoring when I left this morning." His teasing made her heart glow.

"Yeah, right. You're the snorer." After a few more loving jabs at each other, they hung up.

As Courtney got ready to go to the construction site, she wondered how Gary had passed the night. She hoped she could call him for the latest information and update him on the possible pictures from Izzy. She'd have to tell him to keep it to himself. She'd send the pictures to Sheriff Warren or present them to the detectives working the cases.

She was sure if Honor and Janine stole those earrings, Honor hadn't been able to resist wearing them at least once. She wasn't as sure about Janine. She could see her hiding anything she took and pushing it to the back of a drawer, trying to forget about it. And hiding it from Brian, who wasn't as clueless as Doug.

***

Izzy found the pictures around noon and emailed them to Courtney. When she received them, she forwarded them to Sheriff Warren. They were perfect, showing both the watch Izzy mentioned and the earrings. There were also two rings on Valerie's hand and what appeared to be a gold watch on Simon's wrist.

After sending the pictures to the sheriff, the day dragged on and on. She went to the construction site, where Robb worked inside alone, and Luke's crew worked on the roof. The noise annoyed her, even though she knew it meant progress. Her impatience to hear what was happening with Janine and Honor caused her irritation, not the workers.

Alex tried to keep her busy. He must have asked Robb for a bunch of odd jobs for her to do, because she'd finish one thing and they'd have something else for her to do. She completed the latest task and approached Robb. "Thanks for coming on a Sunday. I didn't expect that."

"Someone needed to be around for the Dickinson crew, so here I am. We're getting so close to the weather shutting them down, they're working today. I didn't think they would come, but Luke says it needs to get done before the snow hits on Tuesday."

"Well, I appreciate you coming and taking care of them, and Luke's crew working the extra time to get it done before the snow. I'll have to catch him before they leave or give him a call. I'd rather be out at your farm communing with those little ponies."

He smiled his gentle smile. "Me too. But life goes on, and bills need to be paid. Besides, even petting miniature ponies would bore you after a while. You need more adventure."

She didn't know if she liked that he'd pegged her personality so well, but he was kind. "You're right. I've been called curious, a busybody, and now adventurous. I've probably forgotten a few other qualities people mentioned lately."

"I wouldn't worry about it." He pulled up a board from the floor. "You are unique, and from what I'm hearing, you've done a great service to the community this week."

"I hope so. But I wish they'd hurry up with the official word." She paced back and forth.

"All in good time. We don't want them to slip the net at this point." Robb pulled a nail out of a board.

Courtney's eyes widened. "Hey. Do you like to fish?"

His eyes lit up. "Love it. Haven't done much lately. Need a silent partner."

"Well, there's Ed, but I was thinking of someone else. Johnny expressed an interest. Maybe something to consider when he comes home from his trip. He's quiet."

His eyes twinkled. "Yep, you're a busybody." He held up his hand, halting her protest. "A good one. Yes, and a good idea. I've always liked Johnny. I used to drink too." His voice hinted at some long-ago sadness.

"I'm sorry. You seem to have conquered it and made a good life."

The twinkle came back. "I have. And I'll see if Johnny wants to go fishing when he returns from his trip. Good idea."

"See? Even busybodies have reasons for existing. Now, what's my next project while I wait with curiosity?" She grinned at him.

***

Alex and Courtney decided to attend the Sunday evening church service in Dickinson to avoid any gossip at St. Mary's Church in Elm City. Everyone would ask them questions about the events of the prior day.

The knock on their door at 9:30 was expected. Gary texted he'd stop by and update them on everything he could. When Courtney opened the door, he looked tired but happy.

He stepped in and hugged her before she could even say hello. When he saw Alex behind her, he did the same thing.

Courtney led the way to the living room, not even mentioning refreshments. It was late. No one needed coffee tonight. They had answers, and Gary would fill in the blanks.

"Well, Honor and Janine have been charged with my parents' deaths." He closed his eyes for a moment and opened them. "It feels surreal. Sometimes I doubted this moment would ever come. I am so glad I sold the house to the two of you. Without your help, my parents' killers might have gotten away with murder." He settled deeper into the recliner. "Thank you both for all of your help and patience."

Alex and Courtney glanced at each other and back at Gary. "You're welcome."

"Courtney did most of the work between the two of us," Alex added.

"You did your part, listening to me spout theories." She turned back to Gary. "Tell us what happened."

"Janine admitted she shot Mom and Dad, and Honor was there." His breath hitched. "Doug was framed by Janine for Waylon's death."

Behind his smile, he looked sad and tired. "How did they find enough evidence to arrest Honor and Janine?"

He shook his head at her. "Pictures. I can't believe you thought of them taking and wearing my mom's everyday jewelry. Someone at the police station made the comment she bet Honor actually wore them in public for big occasions if she was sure she'd gotten away with the plan."

Courtney could believe it about Honor.

"The police officer was right. She checked which awards Honor might have received for construction projects in the past eight years or other events that required dressing up. She found a lovely picture of Honor receiving a construction award and wearing the earrings. Some photographer snapped a wonderful color picture and posted it on social media.

"After that, it was easy to get another search warrant for Honor and Doug's house to look specifically for the earrings or other jewels that matched the pictures we received from Izzy. The first warrant was due to the screwdriver with blood on it, and Doug's arrest. Of course, the earrings would have been ignored as unimportant when they executed that warrant.

"As Janine lied about going to Bismarck for a spa day with Honor on the date of their death, and after her extensive confession, they also searched her house." He shook his head again at

Courtney. "You were right. She had the watch with the inscription."

"Did their husbands know what happened?" Alex asked.

"Not at first. They say they never knew, but I wonder if they didn't begin to suspect the past six months. When Doug was framed, he was sure Honor killed Waylon. He said Honor was gone that night, and he'd stayed home. Brian came over, and they played poker."

"Who killed Waylon? Was it both of the women together, like with your parents?" Courtney asked.

"The police did another house-to-house on your block. One of your neighbors mentioned they saw a woman going into Waylon's house shortly before midnight, and she left about ten minutes later. The neighbor said he was shocked because he'd never seen a woman at Waylon's house. He figured Waylon was in love with Patty and would never find another woman."

"Why didn't he tell you all this the first time you canvassed the area?" Courtney leaned forward to catch every word.

"I asked him, but he said he wasn't home the first time we came around, early Thursday morning. We weren't able to get back to him until Saturday. He said he'd planned to tell us, but we got to his house before he called it in. His daughter had a baby that night, which was why he was up pacing around in the first place. He rushed to Dickinson to see the baby early Thursday morning."

Gary's shoulders slumped. "I don't think we would have connected it to Janine. The description of the woman was vague. A woman with light hair, wearing a baseball cap. It was late at night, and he didn't have a good view. Janine has dark hair, but we found a blonde wig at her house. Guess she was double-crossing Honor until she finally lost it and confessed to killing Waylon."

"How did you decide it was Janine?" Alex asked.

"The guy kept watching out the window, said he was relieved to see she left fairly quickly. Guess he really thought Waylon was a stand-up kind of guy and didn't like seeing him have a midnight tryst. Anyway, when the woman came out of Waylon's house, he didn't see Waylon. He watched the woman walk down the sidewalk and realized she hadn't parked in front of Waylon's house, which roused his curiosity again. He saw her go to the end of the block and turn left. By then, he had opened his window and heard a vehicle start up, so he knew she didn't live in the neighborhood.

"The police went around to the block where the guy thought she'd probably parked and discovered someone who'd seen a truck they couldn't identify parked on the street late that night. The witness on that street where the vehicle was parked said she's not good at recognizing models and only knows the vehicles parked regularly on her street."

"Why didn't she say something? I mean, it was the night Waylon was murdered. Why didn't she put it together or at least report it?" Courtney let out a frustrated sigh at the delay.

"Not everyone thinks in terms of suspects, Courtney." Gary and Alex laughed at Gary's words. "Especially a nice eighty-year-old woman who believes nothing bad happens in a small town. She assumed a neighbor had company.

Now, if she had been one of those people who are suspicious of everyone, who knows what would have happened?"

"Oh, fine." She crossed her arms, pretending to be annoyed, but her mind went to other questions. "Janine framed Doug and Honor for Waylon's murder?"

"Looks that way. She changed her statement and admitted she killed him. When she and Brian were out digging for my mom's jewelry, she noticed the hole behind the shed. She said it appeared new, which suggested someone else knew exactly where to dig. She settled on Waylon, because she'd seen his vehicle out on that road late one night when she wanted to dig. Maybe Waylon saw Janine's vehicle, and the same thing occurred to him after the holes were dug. He guessed she was the murderer. Maybe he planned to tell Johnny, and Janine got to him first.

"That's the current guess, and we may never know. Janine claims Waylon didn't deserve the jewels. She'd killed for them before, and she'd kill again." Gary leaned back into the recliner.

Courtney shuddered, remembering Janine's cold stare. She'd gone completely around the bend. "What did Janine say happened the night of your parents' death? Did she say why your parents were killed? I assume your parents would give up the jewels if they were threatened."

Gary's fists clenched in their usual way when he tried to hold in strong emotions. "They took Honor's vehicle. Honor said Janine came up with the plan, but she agreed they wouldn't shoot anyone. They'd take guns to threaten my parents and assumed they would give Honor and Janine the jewelry once they saw the guns. It didn't work out that way.

"Honor and Janine diverge here on their stories. Janine claimed my dad said he wouldn't give them the jewels, and he had a gun too. She said he shot first, and she shot him to stop him but accidentally killed him instead. Honor said Janine deliberately killed my dad to make my mom more likely to give up the jewelry. She even wondered if Janine planned to kill both of them from the beginning of the plan, but Honor said she never would have joined her if she'd known. She didn't kill anyone.

"Honor told the police my mom admitted the gems were buried but became stubborn once

Janine killed my father. Honor could tell there was no way my mom would give them the jewels after that, and Janine just turned and shot her when she realized she'd made Mom too angry to get the jewels."

Courtney watched Gary stoically recite what he'd heard in the interviews. How long would it take for him to let it settle in his mind? She and Alex needed to help him and pray that Gary came to some understanding with God for peace. "What's Janine's version of shooting your mom?"

"She laughed." Gary jumped up from the recliner and paced.

Courtney glanced at Alex, who stood and stretched. "Come on, buddy. Let's take a walk."

"There's some more investigating to conduct and evidence to be gathered, but essentially, the cases are solved. Hopefully, those two women end up in prison. We still don't know what Waylon was going to tell Johnny. I guess that will be a mystery unless Honor or Janine can tell us. We're guessing it's the fact he saw Janine out on the road late at night by your inn when he went to dig up the jewelry."

"What would Honor have done to Janine if she'd found out Janine framed her and Doug for Waylon's murder before they were arrested?" Courtney wanted the end of the story, and Gary seemed to want to tell it. He hadn't taken up Alex's suggestion of a walk.

"Anybody's guess with those two. Anyway, they're behind bars now, and they've let Doug go. He didn't know what they'd done." He stopped pacing and stood in front of the window air conditioner.

"A few more questions, and then you're going for a walk." Alex looked at Courtney. "Ask, and then I'm dragging him out of here."

"What about Brian and Janine and the abuse claims? What happened there?" She also wanted to know about the children.

Gary's shoulders dropped slightly at the change in subject. "Seems Janine was the abuser. Brian has all the scars. She has no injuries. Not a single break or bruise anywhere. They did x-rays and other tests on both of them. They brought Brian in for an interview, and he showed them his back and stomach."

"What happened when the police interviewing her told her they believed Brian?" She wished she'd been there for that moment.

"She rattled her handcuffs and said, 'He can have those three brats. He didn't hurt me. I hurt him.' The look on her face sent chills down my back, and I was behind one-way glass. Those poor children. At least she's out of their life now." He shuddered.

Courtney's stomach turned over. "And the children?"

"They told the social worker that their mother made them go to bed early, which most kids complain about. They also said she didn't feed them some nights or mornings before school. They had to sit quietly in a corner, and if they moved, she'd slap them. I'm sure there was more, but I didn't stay to hear it. It made me sick, and I'd had enough. They've been reunited with their dad." He turned to Alex. "Time for that walk."

"Are you going to stick around Elm City or move on now you know what happened?" Courtney asked as the men headed for the door.

"I'm planning on staying. Maybe someday I'll move, but I kind of like it here. I'll see how it goes in the next year." Gary shrugged.

"And how are you doing with everything?" Courtney asked him.

"I'm tired but satisfied. It's going to take some time for it to sink in that the search is over. A long time to recover." Gary's face was suddenly haggard, his eyes dull.

Courtney had another inspired idea. "What do you think about fishing? I hear it's relaxing."

"Oh, you do, do you?" A slight glimmer of humor appeared in his eyes. "You don't know from personal experience?"

She didn't tell him she didn't like big bodies of water. "When Johnny gets back from his time away, he might take up fishing. And Robb is interested in it too." She smiled.

"You can't keep your hands out of anyone's life, can you?" he marveled.

"Get used to it if you want to stay friends with us," Alex warned. "She's unstoppable when she gets an idea."

"Hey, they're good ideas," she objected.

"They are," Gary agreed.

“Plus, we need to have some further conversations about God. Maybe since things have settled down, you can think about Him in a different way.”

“I’ll talk about it, but no promises.” He threw up his hands in surrender. “I’ll also consider fishing when I have some time off. I’ve traded a lot of shifts lately and have to fill in a lot in the next few weeks for other deputies.”

“No problem. Johnny and Robb can go until you’re ready to join them,” Courtney told him. “And God isn’t going anywhere.”

Alex shook his head. “You’re incorrigible, but I love you.” He kissed her cheek. Then glanced at Gary. “Friends?”

“Friends,” Gary agreed. “But,” he stared at Courtney, “stay out of the rest of my investigations.”

She laughed with him.

EPILOGUE
Five Months Later

Courtney huddled at her usual table in Patty's Diner. Alex came with her because Patty asked them both to join her. The March sunshine shone through the window, highlighting the silverware on the table.

Johnny stood behind the counter, along with Patty. Everyone had gotten used to seeing the two of them together since Christmas. Rumors and guesses floated around about the two of them marrying, but Patty hadn't said anything to her.

"The usual?" Johnny called over to them.

"Yes. Thanks, Johnny."

When Patty came over to their table with coffee and orange juice, Johnny left for the kitchen. "How's business? Any reservations at the Crocus Hill Inn yet?"

Courtney loved how she always called the inn by name instead of saying "the inn."

"Actually, there's been a rush to book lately. They're coming in April."

"About the time we viewed the house last year." Alex exchanged smiles with Courtney.

"You two are the ultimate lovebirds," Patty said. "Always smiling at each other."

They burst into laughter. "We keep up the charade in public. Thanks for the coffee and juice."

"You're welcome. Johnny and I are joining you this morning since everyone has already left. We had our busy time early today. They're checking the cows for calves, hoping the cold doesn't freeze one of the poor things." She turned over the other two cups on their saucers and poured coffee in each. When she sat down, she added cream to hers and stirred.

Johnny came out with everyone's food, and they all enjoyed the meal together. After Patty topped off the cups with coffee, Johnny cleared his throat and gazed down at the table. He continued to display shyness when emotional.

"Patty and I have something to tell you." He reached for Patty's hand, and they intertwined their fingers.

"We're getting married." Patty rummaged in her apron pocket and took out the ring. "I don't wear it at work yet. We wanted to tell you two first, because you were the ones who got us on the right track."

Courtney jumped up and hugged Patty. "Congratulations! You both deserve much happiness." She shook Johnny's sweaty hand. Perspiration beaded on his forehead from either the hot stove or embarrassment. It didn't matter to her.

Alex followed Courtney with a hug for Patty and a handshake for Johnny. "Yes. Congratulations."

"What do you mean we put you on the right track? I mean, we figured out a few things around here, which didn't help you and Patty get together," Alex said.

Johnny turned to Courtney. "Do you remember what you said to me about Lori the day you visited me at the clinic?"

She hid her shiver at the close call she had with Janine. "Yes. I was so proud of you."

"I appreciated that. We discussed Lori's favoritism in brothers. It made me start thinking of Patty. I'd always had a crush on her, and then she dated Waylon. I decided to bury my feelings. After you and I talked, I wondered if maybe Patty could possibly like me, so I worked up my courage and checked with her. Turns out she had a crush on me too." His smile was wider than hers.

"Great." Her eyes met Patty's. "Everything works out."

"It sure does."

The love in her eyes when she gazed at Johnny was obvious and had been obvious for months to those around them.

"When's the wedding?" Courtney asked.

"Next week," Patty answered.

Courtney's mouth dropped open. "What?"

"A simple ceremony in Dickinson. Would you two like to be our matron of honor and groomsman and witnesses? We're only inviting Johnny's family and you two."

Courtney glanced at Alex, who nodded enthusiastically. "Definitely. We'll be there!" he said.

Later, she and Alex arrived at their home at Crocus Hill Inn. The week before, they'd moved into one of the apartments on the second floor.

Finishing touches were being completed on the first floor, but they were close to having the inn completely redone.

"So, we're hiring Braden for grounds work and maintenance and Skyler for housekeeping? And Willow for cooking? Did we miss anything?"

They sat in their living room with its wide-open floor plan into the kitchen. She studied the black-and-cream plaid couch and the cream-colored pillow with a picture of a black Scottish terrier printed on both sides. Then she looked at Alex. "We have a home again."

He pulled her closer on the couch and hugged her. "Wherever you are is home to me. But I do have to say, the heat works better here than at the house on Sunflower Lane."

She laughed.

~~~

Check out the next book in the Crocus Hill Inn series
THE LAST SCAM - Book 2
~~~

Courtney and Alex greet their first guests at Crocus Hill Inn. But are they really there for the wonderful program Courtney has set up to help people? Or are they there for their own sinister purposes? Once more, Courtney finds herself in the middle of an investigation, this time to save the reputation of the inn.

Picture of Book 2 – *The Last Scam*
https://www./jeanrezab.com

BELLA'S COOKIES

¾ cup butter
1 cup flour
1 cup oatmeal
½ cup cocoa
2 eggs
3 tsp cinnamon
½ tsp baking soda
¾ tsp baking powder
2 tsp vanilla
1 cup vanilla chips
1 ½ cup milk chocolate chips

Drop by tablespoon 6-8 in pan.
Bake at 350 degrees for 12 minutes.
Let sit on pan for 1 minute before moving.

Enjoy!

ACKNOWLEDGMENTS

God has blessed me with the right people for this writing adventure and deserves the glory for giving me ideas and the ability to write, and the courage to continue improving my craft to write more impactful stories that help others.

Special thanks to the excellent editor, Krista Venero, at Mountains Wanted Publishing & Indie Author Services for great suggestions. She helped create a better book than I could have envisioned on my own.

Thank you to the book cover artist at SunsetRoseBooks.com for an amazing cover.

Considerable thanks to my family who have encouraged me in my writing journey.

Thank you to Chanda for reading the book and her helpful comments. Thank you to Sally and Ruth, my first writing friends, who continue to encourage me along this winding road of publishing and writing. Thank you to Jann, who is great at bouncing ideas around. Also, thanks to the Wordsmiths critique group who continue to remain part of my writing journey. And last, but not least, thank you to the Optimistic Writers who continue to provide writing, marketing, and all-around advice on what is currently happening in the writing world. I couldn't have finished this book without everyone's help.

Special thanks to Connie Victoria Volk for helping by proofreading and making suggestions for a stronger book.

A special thank you to Bella for Bella's Cookies' recipe. She's a wonderful girl with a beautiful imagination and tasty cookies.

Also by Jean Rezab

Crocus Hill Inn Mysteries
The Last Owners
The Last Scam
The Last Cake

Richmond Sibling Series
Chokecherry Valley Comfort
Chokecherry Valley Joy
Chokecherry Valley Love
Chokecherry Valley Faith
Chokecherry Valley Collection

Standalones
In This Place Together (Biblical)
The Prediction (Mystery)

ABOUT THE AUTHOR

Jean Rezab writes from her home in North Dakota. She loves the wide-open prairie and spring wildflowers. She's an avid mystery reader. An excerpt of her work has appeared in ND Humanities Magazine.

Visit her website https://www.jeanrezab.com